DEDICATION

For the honor and glory of God
in honor of Jesus, Mary, Joseph,
and all the angels,

*   *   *

In thanksgiving to God
for my husband, Michael
and all of our children,

*   *   *

To Mary Kay,
who signed her name, "Sarah"
in the concrete.

ACKNOWLEDGEMENTS

I wish to say "thank you" first

to Our Lord and Our Lady

To my husband, Michael

for his encouragement and guidance.

To my publisher, Jim Gilboy, and CMJ Associates.

To Ronda, Trish, and Amy

for their diligent work and support.

And to all my family

who helped me with insight and memories.

Even though I drew from

some life experiences,

the characters in this book are fictional.

Places and circumstances are coincidental.

Chapter 1

It was hot and humid, and the sun was starting to set as Sheila drove her car right up to the curb, parked, and shut the motor off. She sat there in front of her adobe home and felt the fatigue and the strain of the last few months overwhelm her.

Home at last, where she had longed to be. Yet, instead of hurrying inside, she found herself sitting in her car, reflecting on her memories. Where could her identical twin sister, Sarah, be? Why did they have to be separated all these years?

As soon as she learned that she had a twin sister who was missing, she took action. Unfortunately, the detective agency she hired several months ago could find no trace of her sister. Why did she find that hard to comprehend? After all, hadn't her parents hired several detective agencies for the same purpose all those years ago?

Still, after twenty-one years, no one could find Sarah, so why did she presume that she could do it? Yet she did. With all her heart she believed she could, and now. . . .

I must stop berating myself. I've done my best. Why can't I stop thinking about her over and over? What is she like? Are we really identical? Has she been treated well all these years or has she been afraid and lonely or abused? Where is she now, while I am going through this torment? Is she happy?

Stop this, once and for all! she thought. She pushed her auburn hair back and pressed her hand to her forehead as if this gesture would banish the anguish and distress she felt.

This last trip had been exhausting. When the agency called and said they had received their best lead yet, she was sure they had found her sister. She was elated and couldn't wait to go. She left at once for Santa Barbara, California to meet her sister. Unfortunately, she went, only to be heartbroken once again.

On this trip, more than any of the other trips she had taken, she felt confident that they had found her. The photograph they showed her of the woman and so much of the detailed report she had received filled her with hope and a false sense of security.

It was uncanny, she had to admit. Even when she met this woman in person, Sheila thought she might be her real sister, if she and Sarah were not identical.

Sheila was tall and slender with a natural confidence. She had greenish-gray eyes that were very warm and friendly, her complexion light with a tinge of rose on her cheeks, her lips full and shapely. She had thick, smooth auburn hair, shoulder-length, and turned in a slight page. She used very little make-up, only lipstick and a light powder base.

She couldn't help but think how much this woman resembled her, except that her hair was shorter and more of a sandy color, without the deep reddish tones of auburn she had. Still, their features, skin and eyes, were so close. . . . But the woman did not have the "scotty dog" birthmark above her right ankle. The birthmark her real sister would have. Her mother told her that they were both born with it. Her birthmark was an inch to an inch and a half in size, and light tan in color. Someone would have to know it was there, but if you looked carefully you could see the shape of the ears and tail, the tiny legs. It was undoubtedly a "scotty dog".

She didn't know how many minutes went by before she forced herself to unbuckle her seatbelt, open the door, and slide out of her lovely blue Mercedes. Walking slowly toward the wooden gate that led into the courtyard, she pulled her purse open to search for her house keys. It had been so long since she used them and she was fumbling. Finally, she stood still and, in the dusk, tried to see inside her purse. As she reached for the keys, she realized she was shaking.

Why am I trembling like this? she thought. Maybe her brother, Richard, was right when he had suggested that either he or Leah, her older sister, or both of them, should meet her in Albuquerque. Richard didn't like it one bit that she had moved to Santa Fe and lived alone.

They had always been so close, the three of them. Richard entered the medical field in their father's footsteps and Leah followed him. They were both surprised when Sheila wasn't interested in medicine as a career.

After two years of college, she decided not to go back for awhile, but instead, move to Santa Fe. Richard was the only one who fought her on it. Everyone objected at first, but he persisted. She could hear his protests now.

"New Mexico? You want to move to Santa Fe, alone? You're only twenty years old. What's wrong with Arizona, with Phoenix, where you have lived all your life? Your family is here, your friends are here. You don't know anyone in Santa Fe and you'll be about six hundred miles away from us. That's no stone's throw. What if you need us? You're very vulnerable, you know."

She smiled now as she remembered how vehement he was. He was always there for her, like wanting to meet tonight when she got back to New Mexico. He had called her in Santa Barbara before she left for Los Angeles to get her flight.

"Hi, sis, listen. Leah and I want to meet your plane. Then you won't have to drive your car back into Santa Fe alone. I'll be there and I'll drive. We can all catch up on what you have found out, and you'll feel better having us there for you. It'll be late when you get in. The family doesn't feel good about your being alone."

Five minutes after she hung up with Richard, Sue, her sister-in-law, called. "Sheila, don't be so stubborn. Richard really wants to be there and I don't mind at all. I think, after these trying few months, it would be good for the three of you to be together."

She remembered distinctly her reaction was a vehement outburst. "No, no, I don't want anyone with me! I want to be alone!"

Now, however, as she found herself standing in front of the door, she just couldn't bring herself to put the key in the lock and open it. Instead, she turned and looked at her lovely little courtyard. Richard must have hired someone to keep it up while she was gone. The flowers were beautiful, sitting in flower boxes around the cobblestones, and up on the window sills. The small amount of grass she had was just mowed and looked so green; it had that good, fresh-cut smell to it. The chairs and small table were still in the same place. She thought of the tranquillity that so often accompanied her, when she strolled around the courtyard and puttered with her flowers. Although she had a woman come in and do the cleaning and the cooking for her, she did her own yard work, except for the mowing and trimming. She enjoyed taking care of her plants and flowers. It was a form of relaxation that gave her peace and serenity.

Serenity. She had lost it for a while, but now it was coming back and giving her courage. She inserted the key and opened the door. Then, without giving another thought to her situation, she went around turning lights on, putting things down or moving them from here to there, as though she had never been away.

Even here, in the house, she could see Richard's loving touch. Flowers with a card saying "Welcome Home" were perched on the dining room table. Emma, her housekeeper, must have been here when they were delivered. Thinking of Richard, she could almost feel his presence. If he and Leah had been here, they could have stayed up all night and talked.

Sheila sat down on the couch, put her feet up on the ottoman and laid her head back. As she closed her eyes, vivid pictures came and went, fleetingly, through her mind.

Sweet Leah, her sister, whom she dearly loved. Leah looked so much like their mother, Ellen. They were a little shorter than she, but slim and attractive, with light brown hair and hazel eyes. Leah had an ivory complexion that was flawless and full curved lips like hers. Leah and Ellen both had short hair with hints of auburn in it and they had it feathered back off their faces.

Sheila remembered how Leah would always try to be a little mother to her, protecting her when she was small. Even when she got older and started dating, Leah would tell her, "Don't be late. Be careful where he takes you. Remember to be good." She was always there with advice and she was always willing to listen and offer her help. At nineteen, Leah had been engaged to Joseph. Sheila would never forget Joe. He had been thoughtful and kind. He had been a pilot for a major airline and was killed in a plane crash a week before his and Leah's wedding. They had been deeply in love and his death was devastating for Leah and for the rest of the family. They did not know how to help her.

Sheila remembered how much she hurt for Leah. She would never forget the suffering they all went through, but for Leah, it was unbearable. She cried and cried, she wouldn't eat or sleep.

Ellen tried to console her, telling her, "Even though you will always love Joe and this suffering seems like it will never pass, as time goes by it will get better. You will heal. Please, let me help you, let God help you."

Sheila could almost hear, once again, Leah's response. "I'll never marry. I'll never know a man like Joe again. He is the one I loved and always will love."

Later, Sheila heard her mother and father talking. "Don't worry, Howard," Ellen said. "It will take time. Leah is strong and some-day, she will meet someone who will be able to take her hurt away." That was six years ago and Leah still had not yet met anyone she cared for, even though she dated on and off.

She had a very nice condominium near the hospital where her internship was. She was contented now, with her work, college, friends and family. Sheila's thoughts returned to herself.

She was only twenty-one years old, and here she was, living in Santa Fe, New Mexico. She had her own house and car. She re-membered the week her mother and father helped her move all her belongings from their home in Phoenix, where she was born and raised. Her mother and Leah came over from Phoenix for two weeks to help her pick out all the furnishings.

Mother and Dad had been so good about helping her move when she was not quite twenty-one. They didn't fully understand her at the time, but they helped her buy the house, furnish it, and settle in. However, Sheila made them promise that when she re-ceived her trust fund from her grandparents, they would let her pay back everything. After all, she could well afford to, she would re-ceive over one million dollars when she turned twenty-one.

Her plan, as she tried to explain to them, was to move to Santa Fe and start to work on being a writer. She also wanted to begin looking into journalism as a career. She wanted to do this, instead of going to college all day. She would take college courses that were necessary for what she wanted to do, but there was no hurry. Instead, living in Santa Fe, becoming part of the culture, being ex-posed to the people, that was what was in her heart. That's what she needed to become a writer. Life experience, and being part of these people, a part of this world, here in New Mexico was what she wanted.

As a little girl, she had fallen in love with Santa Fe when her parents brought the whole family here on vacation or to Taos on ski-ing trips. Her thoughts switched back to Richard, his wife, Sue, and her precious nieces, Cynthia, who was four, and Lisa, who was two-and-a-half. She just loved them both so dearly and was always eager to be with them whenever she went home to Phoenix for a visit. Because of her search for her sister, her visits home had been frequent recently.

She had been away from her own home for quite a while. After each heartbreaking trip in the last six months, she never came back to Santa Fe. Instead, she would go right on to Phoenix to see her parents, Richard, Sue and the children, and Leah. Then they would talk at length about where she had been, what clues she had found. Over and over again, they would rehash everything.

Her parents would admonish her to give up, that she had to let the idea of finding Sarah go. They knew what she was going through, they, too—

What bell was that? Sheila thought, startled back from her memories. The ringing was incessant. "The doorbell," she said, out loud, as she jumped up from the couch and headed for the door.

"Who is it?" she asked, and heard right away the familiar voice of Leah. She opened the door and they were instantly in each other's arms, both of them crying and holding on to each other as though they had been separated for years.

Sheila said, through her sobs, "Leah, this time I thought we had found her! The detective agency was positive, it all seemed so promising. I can't tell you how empty I feel now. All of you are right. I have to stop this, I have to stop looking." Sheila, who had been saying this with such anguish, abruptly pulled herself together. Looking into Leah's beautiful hazel eyes, she said in a much softer and calmer voice, "I'm so glad you're here. Let's make some hot tea and get ready for bed."

Leah was all set for this suggestion. She had been driving for about ten hours from Phoenix, so she could be here when Sheila was due to get home. She now studied her younger sister and thought how very much she loved her. There were four years difference in their ages, Leah being the older, and yet, they had always been the best of friends.

As they both were getting undressed and ready for that cup of chamomile tea, Sheila's thoughts were those of thanks to God for sending Leah to her tonight. She thanked Him fervently that Leah had not listened to her earlier outburst, in which she said she did not want any of them to be with her.

Thank God, she thought, for a family who understands you, even when you do not understand yourself.

She came back from her reverie when Leah said, "Wherever you are in your thoughts, Sheila, I want to hear and share them all. Now come on, let's pour that tea and curl up on the couch and talk."

For a few moments, they sipped their tea in silence. Sheila began, "My heart was pounding when the detective had me meet Emily, the woman whom they thought was Sarah. Emily told them she was sure she did not have a sister she knew nothing about. They insisted she at least meet me. They told her that Sarah wouldn't know she had been abducted. I think they made her feel sorry for me, so she finally gave in to their request. She explained to me how hesitant she was. Oh, Leah, I can't begin to tell you how I felt." She swallowed and pressed her lips together.

Leah reached for her hand and patted it. "Honey, it's okay. Everything is okay now. I know how hard this must have been for you. My heart aches when I think of what you have suffered these last few months. The whole family can't stop worrying about you."

"I'm all right," Sheila said with a deep sigh. "As soon as Emily and I met, I knew she wasn't our sister Sarah. It was such a disappointment, I could hardly keep myself from falling apart. Emily and I visited for a short while. My heart pounded the whole time. The detective was very apologetic. He really felt bad. I told him it wasn't their fault. I wanted to make the trip to see for myself if this woman was my sister. I also told them I wouldn't need their services any longer. Leah, I can't go through this again. I'm going to stop searching."

Leah was delighted. "Sheila, I am so happy. I can't wait to call Mom and Dad. All the family will be as relieved as I am." They hugged each other good night. Leah was ready to get settled in her room. She was exhausted.

Long after Leah had gone off to sleep, Sheila lay awake, wide awake, remembering once again the moment she received the letter from the bank. The memories came flooding back painfully, as though they were happening all over again.

She had gone home to Phoenix for the holidays. She needed to get the trust fund settled and have the money put in her own name. Her father had chosen the bank. He was also setting up how much money she should invest. She was happy he was taking care of all of this; she knew nothing about finances.

She had thought she would be able to receive her trust fund right on her twenty-first birthday, which was August 24, 1995, but she hadn't heard anything until January fifth of the following year. How vividly she remembered the day she opened the letter from the bank. She was reading it as she slowly walked through the house toward the back patio and yard, where her mother was trying to plant a new rose bush. The ache in her heart was coming back as she lay awake and vividly remembered the awful moment.

The letter said that her checks would be sent to her as soon as her accounts were opened, and that they appreciated her business. But then she stopped reading, confused by the next sentence. What were they talking about? Who were they talking about? The letter went on to say that if Sarah did not claim her trust fund by her thirtieth birthday, then Sarah's money would be deposited into Sheila's account. Sheila would be the sole beneficiary of the second trust fund, which was also valued at over one million dollars. In addition, the fund would be accumulating interest for the next eight years, or until the matter was resolved.

Coming onto the patio, Sheila innocently asked, "Mother, who is Sarah?"

Ellen froze, dropped the spade, and turned slowly to stare at Sheila. In almost a whisper, she asked, "Sheila, where did you hear that name?"

Her mother was ashen and visibly shaken. Sheila didn't understand. "Mother, what's wrong? Are you all right? Should I call Father to come home?"

Dropping the letter and running to her mother's side, she tried to help her to a chair. Ellen started crying and she couldn't talk. Every time she tried, nothing would come out.

Sheila could still see herself calling for Martha the housekeeper, who had always been with their family.

"Martha, help me! Please, help me! There is something terribly wrong with Mother! All I did was ask her who Sarah was, and she. . . ." Sheila stopped abruptly as she heard Martha gasp and then quickly put her hand over her mouth.

"Oh, no,. . . how do you know about Sarah?" she had asked. Martha was short and heavyset but not fat. she had white hair and wore it pulled back with a bun at the nape of her neck. She always looked clean and neat and had an aura of calmness about her. She was a pleasant, no-nonsense person who rarely showed her love outwardly, but the children knew it was always there. She was precious to the children who, as they were growing up, would spend a lot of time talking with her in the kitchen or in the laundry room or yard. It was she who would make them pick up their toys before bed and help them say a good-night prayer. They loved her dearly.

Even though she was so frightened for her mother and did not understand anything of what was going on, Sheila took control and told Martha, "Get Daddy now! Tell him to come right home! I mean it, Martha, get my dad!" With that, she helped Ellen into the house.

It seemed like an eternity, but actually it was only about twenty-five minutes before Howard was beside his wife and daughter. The three women had been waiting patiently for him to arrive, each engrossed in her own thoughts.

Several times, Sheila tried to talk to her mother, but all Ellen would respond with was, "Wait for your father. He will explain."

Martha poured a glass of wine and kept trying to get Ellen to sip it. Ellen seemed nervous every time she glanced at Sheila, who was studying her intently.

Not knowing what else to say to help her mother, Sheila's own thoughts were racing wildly. They had been ever since Ellen's reaction to the letter and the name Sarah. All of a sudden, the thought came to her: Where is the letter? I remember I dropped it when Mother looked like she was going to faint.

Looking around, she remembered being on the patio. She went outside once again and, sure enough, there it was, right next to the rose bush. She had finished recovering it and was back with Ellen when her Dad, who had just arrived, was asking, "Ellen, are you all right?"

Before he could finish, Ellen was sobbing in his arms and it was Sheila who blurted out, "Daddy, who is Sarah?"

Once again the room was filled with tension. Howard and Ellen just looked at each other and the look in their eyes brought a lump into Sheila's throat. Ellen, who sensed her daughter's apprehension and had somewhat gained her own composure, was quick to say, "Howard, before we talk with Sheila, we must have Richard, Leah, and Sue come over so we can explain to them all at the same time who Sarah is." Turning to Martha, she requested, "Please call Richard and tell him. . . ."

Howard, holding her gently in his arms, whispered, "No, Ellen, I'll call Richard and ask him to have them all come over here as soon as possible. He will find Leah." Then almost in the same breath, he turned back to Martha. "Please just continue in your regular duties as much as you are able today, Martha, and perhaps have something light to eat and coffee made for later. I'm sure everyone will appreciate some hot coffee." He tried to give her a weak smile of assurance, hugged Ellen, and left the room.

Gaining strength from her beloved husband's courage, Ellen went directly to Sheila, put her arms around her, and said, "Darling, we love you so much. Be patient, just a little longer, and your father and I will try to explain everything." Her voice broke several times. Letting her arm drop to Sheila's waist, they moved toward the parlor. They both sat and waited, each lost in the silence of her own emotions.

Richard and Sue had only been there a few minutes when Leah came hurrying into the room, her face full of concern and worry. Howard kept trying to reassure everyone that everything was all right. He asked them to sit down and listen to what he had to say. "Please, all of you, listen and try not to interrupt me until I have finished, for this is going to be very hard for your mother and me, as well as for each of you."

He walked over to where Ellen was sitting on the love seat and as he sat beside her, their hands instantly came together. With the other hand, Ellen was clutching a handkerchief and kept dabbing her eyes with it. Howard cleared his throat and he was visibly shaken as he said, "Richard, you were only six and Leah was four when your sister, Sheila, was born. What we did not tell any of you,. . ." He cleared his throat and, looking directly into Sheila's eyes, he paused momentarily before he spoke.

"Sheila, you have a twin sister, Sarah."

He could not go on. Each of his children gasped with disbelief that they knew nothing of this. How could they? Why weren't they told? Where is she? What happened to her?

They had so many questions and they were so dumbfounded that it took much effort on Howard's part to get everyone's attention again. He insisted, "This is going to be very hard for your mother and me. We need your understanding. We struggled over whether we should tell each one of you. We decided that it would only open too many wounds each time one of you reached an age when we felt you were old enough to be told. We would have to repeat what we are about to tell you now. The suffering and the hurt have been with your mother and me and the rest of the family for over twenty-one years now. I know what you're thinking, that you're all certainly old enough now. You're right; we have talked about it being time. We kept putting it off. Now, it is too late. You found out very unexpectedly about your sister, Sarah, which of course, makes it harder on all of us."

Choking up, he could not go on. He and Ellen gently put their foreheads together in a tender gesture. Their tears merged as they clung together for a few moments.

No one said a word. All of them had tears flowing down their cheeks. They couldn't help themselves. They had never seen their parents like this. There were a few moments of stunned silence until Howard, after wiping his eyes and blowing his nose, continued his heartbreaking story to his shocked and saddened children.

"Sarah and Sheila were born on August 24, 1974. On August twenty-eighth, the day before your mother and the babies were to come home, Sarah was taken from the hospital. When we were told, we were frantic. We offered rewards. We prayed together. All of our family and friends prayed for us and for Sarah.

"On the twenty-ninth, we received a call from a young girl saying she needed money and she had Sarah. She sounded so scared. The phone went dead right after that. We realized she knew our baby's name, Sarah Farrell, from the identification bracelet the hospital puts on newborn babies.

"On the thirtieth, I brought your mother and Sheila home and what should have been a joyous day was one of the dreariest days of our lives. We were torn between being happy and grateful to still have Sheila and devastated at losing Sarah." Howard's voice broke and he could not go on for several minutes.

All this time, Ellen sat quietly, crying and dabbing at her eyes, as her husband valiantly told the children the painful story they had been living with all through the years. Before he went on, Sheila moved close to her parents. She took their hands and they could see that she was visibly shaken and pale. She thought she was dreaming, until once again, she heard her father's voice.

"Two weeks later, she called. 'I'm afraid because of what I've done. Your baby is okay. I'm giving her to someone who will love her and always take good care of her. Forgive me.' Then the phone went dead.

"Once again, the call had not been able to be traced. She had been so brief before quickly hanging up. We have never heard another word in all these years. We have always searched and when any kind of a lead turned up, we always followed through on it.

"Your mother became so ill from depression. For several months, she was listless and didn't know how she could go on, not knowing where her baby was. We both went through a great deal of suffering, wondering about Sarah's welfare. Had she been harmed in any way? Such thoughts obsessed us, especially in the first few months after her abduction. We knew, though, that somehow, we had to go on. We had all of you. We were a family. I told Mother she could not give up. She had all of you to live for. I told her how much we all needed her. The newspapers and broadcast media told of how Sarah Farrell, one of Doctor and Mrs. Farrell's twin daughters had been abducted. They said that I was a prominent surgeon in Phoenix and that we were offering rewards for any information. As I already have told you, we did receive bits of information, all through the years. Your mother and I would leave you for a few days and follow up on these leads, but they proved to be of no avail."

Ellen finally could keep still no longer. "Please forgive us. We did what we thought was best at the time. We have lived in fear of this moment. We always continued to hope and pray that when you heard of Sarah, it would be because we had found her and you were seeing her for the first time. Our prayer all through these years has been that we would be reunited as a family and all of this heartache would have a happy ending."

With this last sentence from Ellen, they were all on their feet, hugging and kissing each other. They were still a family and they could go on together now, even with the impact of this new situation. Now they, too, would help carry the hurt and go on living one day at a time.

With these troubling thoughts churning in her mind, it was morning by the time Sheila finally was able to fall asleep. The last thing she remembered was the rose bush her mother was planting the day the letter arrived.

Chapter 2

Leah took a week off from her college classes and from her job in the hospital. She wanted to spend the week with Sheila. She was happy she hadn't listened to her sister when Sheila said she didn't want anyone with her. They enjoyed the whole time together. During the week, they made several calls to the family in Phoenix, going over again the details of the still fruitless search for Sarah.

Knowing that Howard and Ellen had searched for Sarah unsuccessfully all through the years and that Sheila's untiring search had also not been fruitful, the Farrell family came to the conclusion that their lives must go on as before. It was time to settle once again into their normal daily routines. As the week went on and all this painful sharing kept coming to the surface, Leah was there for Sheila. She loved her sister more than ever for it.

The day after Leah left, Sheila went back to her part-time job on the newspaper, writing human interest columns. She wrote about people who told her how good came out of so many difficult situations in their lives. One column was about a girl who told Sheila that she had been a drug addict, so far gone there didn't seem to be any help for her. Her mother started praying and asked her to pray to the holy angels to change her life. At first, she wouldn't do it. When her mother bought her a guardian angel medal and tearfully implored her to ask for help, she was touched by something deep within. So she simply said each day, "Good holy angel, if you're there, help me." It took a year of suffering with many falls and false starts, but now she was a happy, well-adjusted young lady. Through everything she experienced, she never forgot her promise to say at least once each day, "Good holy angel, if you're there, help me."

Although the stories were often painful, Sheila found them inspiring. She would interview the person, take careful notes, and later, write their story. She loved her work because she met so many interesting people who had changed their lives by the grace of God.

It was now early August. On the twenty-fourth, it would be her twenty-second birthday. She was going home for the occasion, as her mother was planning a whole week, filled with dinners and birthday surprises. Sheila was looking forward to the time with her family. She wanted them to know that she was trying to let Sarah go from her thoughts a little more every day. She would never forget her, of course, but for her own good and for the good of the family, she, too, must let her dream of reuniting with her sister fade.

One evening, she decided to call and tell them her feelings. "Mom, I could not wait for my visit to tell you and Dad some of what is in my heart. Will you have Dad get on the other phone? After a brief pause and an affectionate greeting from her father, she went on. "We have all been so distraught over the last few months and talked so much about Sarah ever since Richard, Leah, and I learned of her existence. The time has come to give it a rest. I understand now how you and mother had to do the very same thing." She had to stop as Ellen broke in.

"Oh, Sheila, do you see that we had to let go, so we could go on with our lives? We couldn't find her , we had not a clue. . . ."

Howard had gone over to Ellen, and put his arms around her. He said, "Ellen, dear, everything is fine. That is what Sheila is trying to tell us. Let her finish." Then right into the mouthpiece, with his voice more than a little hoarse, he urged, "Go on, Sheila."

"Well, what I am trying to say is that now that I am aware of all you both went through, I forgive you for not telling me that I had an identical twin because really, there is nothing to forgive. You did what you thought was best, that is all any of us can do. Now I know the depth of your suffering because I've been through it myself. It's time for me to stop looking for her. I've already told the detective agency to stop. I want to comfort you and Dad so much. Mother, I want you to feel my arms around you both, even though we are so far away. Sarah is in the past and life must go on. I wanted to say this before I came home for my birthday, so that now we can go on with the rest of our lives."

Howard was the first to speak. "Sheila, you will never know how much this means to your mother and me. We have been so worried about you. Understandably, Richard and Leah have been able to accept all of this a lot sooner than you have. We feel the reason is that both of you were in the womb together."

Ellen and Howard were holding hands and she was looking at him with deep feeling. Ellen spoke. "Sheila, we can't wait for the end of the month for you to be with us and for things to be as they used to. Thank you, darling, for calling us. We love you so much."

As they said good-bye and hung the phone up, each one of them took a deep breath and knew that this was a new beginning.

Although Sheila did not fully understand the depths of her emotions about New Mexico, one thing she did know—she loved it. She felt like she had come home ever since moving to Santa Fe. Even as a child, she was determined that someday she would live in New Mexico and be a part of it. One of the things she vividly remembered was all of those trips to Taos. How much she loved the wide open spaces, the countryside, mountains, and sheer beauty of the Rio Grande canyon and river. Even here, in Santa Fe, the mountains were so beautiful and peaceful and green.

Looking at the mountains always gave her peace. With the seasons, the changes in the mountains, the colors they would take on, always made her heart sing. The old town itself inspired her. She loved the shops, the way you could walk and be in the heart of things happening around you. Especially around the plaza. Santa Fe meant "City of Faith". Sheila felt good about it; she wanted to live here. She was thankful.

Wednesday, August seventh dawned just like any other day, so Sheila was completely unprepared for the events that would unfold.

It was such a beautiful morning, she decided to walk to the Gazette, the newspaper she worked for. The day was warm. There was a light breeze that blew through her lovely auburn hair and felt so good. She briskly walked along Water Street toward the newspaper building.

Looking up for just a moment at the sky, she noticed, with great pleasure, the little clusters of rainclouds. They were so pretty this morning. She came back to reality, very suddenly, when she tripped. A man's arms encircled and caught her before she fell. She was so engrossed in the clouds and their beauty, that it was too late for her to stop herself from falling.

She heard his clear vibrant, masculine voice at the same time she felt his arms encircle her. "Hey, there, be careful, young lady."

Sheila's face flushed with embarrassment as she realized people were looking at them with little smiles forming at the corner of their lips. No wonder, she thought, as she became aware that they were both standing like statues and looking into each other's eyes. His arms were still around her.

She moved slightly to release his grasp and he instantly stepped back. "Are you all right, Miss?" he asked. "I'm sorry I held you like that, but for a moment, I thought I recognized you."

Sheila was still a little breathless, yet she smiled a friendly warm smile as she looked directly into this young man's hazel-blue eyes. Her heart and mind were racing for a few seconds as she wondered how she could prolong this encounter long enough to be able to meet him. She felt the stirring of butterflies in her stomach.

She couldn't believe it as she heard herself saying, "I'm fine and I beg your pardon. It shows you what can happen when you're not looking where you're going."

He kept staring at her intently and an uncomfortable silence engulfed them for a second or two. He broke it finally with, "I hate to just walk on after our most unusual meeting. Would you consider it too bold of me if I asked that we meet again this afternoon and get to know each other?" He went on, "I know, how about saying you'll meet me at the La Fonda Hotel in the La Fiesta lounge; say around four p.m.?"

A slight laugh bubbled out of Sheila as she said, "I'd like that."

"Good!" he responded with an enthusiasm that was catching. "My name is Steve Reed and you are. . .?"

This is like a dream, she thought, as she held her hand out. He grasped it with a strength that made her almost wince. "Sheila Farrell. I'm happy we took the time to introduce ourselves and I'll be looking forward to this afternoon."

That was it! They smiled at each other and then went on in different directions. Sheila did not know how he felt, but she was excited. She felt a joy and an anticipation she had not felt for a long time.

Sheila had dated on and off in Phoenix, but nothing serious developed with anyone. It only took one date or two at the most to find out what they really wanted, either her or her money, or both. Her family were Christians and as a young girl she was taught that there were morals in this world that God expected us to follow. A set of rules He had made for us. Purity, honesty, integrity, sincerity. Even at an early age, she wanted to follow them. Many of her friends ignored these rules completely as though there were no God. She believed in Him. She believed in her conscience because whenever she would be tempted to sin, she heard within her a voice telling her what was right or wrong. Some of the young men she had dated really turned her off. They did not seem to understand the kind of love she was looking for.

This was the first time in Santa Fe that anyone had asked her out for a date that she had accepted. She really didn't want to go out with anyone, until now. Yet here she was, meeting a complete stranger and feeling so happy.

She couldn't help think how handsome he was, tall, about six feet, with a nice build, thick brown hair and hazel-blue eyes. His smile was big and warm. She was anxious to see him again.

I hope this day flies, she caught herself thinking as she entered the newspaper building.

On this same morning, in Velarde, a small farming community about forty miles north of Santa Fe, a young woman was running and singing along the edge of the Rio Grande. Her heart was so happy. Her auburn hair blew back in the wind and she resembled a graceful filly as she ran. She was slim and beautiful, with straight long hair reaching halfway down her back. It was full of highlights that shimmered in the sun. Her lips were full and naturally red, her eyes a gray-green. She wore a pretty soft rose-color blouse and a denim blue skirt that went well below her knees. Her right leg, just above her ankle, had a light beige spot about an inch and a half wide. It hadn't tanned like the rest of her legs. No one, without looking closer, could see that it was a birthmark.

Her voice echoed out into the canyons of northern New Mexico and finally, out of breath, she dropped to her knees right in the river.

She laughed. The water felt so good, so cold and fresh. She splashed her face and her dark, tanned skin glowed in the sunlight. In a whisper that was clear as a bell, she said, "Thank you, God, for this day. I give you thanks and praise. My heart and soul sing unto You." Then taking a breath, she added, "Dearest Mother of God, and my mother, help me live each day for God and for you."

With her eyes closed and her face lifted slightly toward the sky, she sat back on her bended knees and silently prayed for the world, her parents and neighbors, and for all those special people who had asked for her prayers during the week. She thought of each one of them, of their personal and temporal needs, but most especially, of their spiritual needs. Twenty or thirty minutes passed. She did not seem at all concerned about time. Thoughts of each individual person she prayed for passed through her mind and heart as she knelt there. She could feel their needs, their sufferings, their joys. Sometimes, she would smile slightly, and then, her smile would instantly turn to tears that slowly rolled down her cheeks.

She seemed unaware of these affects. After her prayer, she splashed happily and enjoyed the water as it swirled swiftly over her legs. She seemed in no hurry. She slowly got up. She was holding her skirt and trying to wring out some of the water. She walked over to a good-sized boulder and sat on it. Her eyes moved along the swiftly moving river, then to the sky and the mountains. Song burst forth from her once again as she gathered herself up and started for home.

Sarah loved her home in Velarde, New Mexico, which was south of where the Rio Grande and Embudo River come together. She lived here with her parents, Carmen and Ernest Montoya. Their's was a small pleasant home, with two bedrooms, a cozy living room, a kitchen with a nice dining area, and one bathroom.

The house was tan stucco over adobe, with wood framed windows and wood lintels over the door and windows. It had a pitched gable roof and corrugated galvanized roofing. A pleasant wood-decked front porch with a wood railing made of latillas and a shed-type roof extended from the main house. It was a little run-down and in need of some stucco and roof repairing and painting. It was back off a gravel road with a gravel driveway to the house. In the front yard there was a statue of Our Lady of Guadalupe. There was a metal swing and a pair of wooden rocking chairs on the porch, from which the family derived much pleasure. About one hundred feet behind the house, there was a thirty by fifty foot pole barn with galvanized tin siding and roofing.

Her mother, Carmen, kept their home so clean. They all worked together on the small farm which barely scratched out a living for them, but nothing hindered their happiness.

Carmen was attractive with short dark brown curly hair, wide brown eyes and a lovely smile that lit up her face. Her skin was firm, with very few wrinkles. She was of medium height and build, full of energy with a personality that was warm and compassionate. She always had a desire to be of service to her family and others whenever they needed anything.

Sarah often thought how she and her parents were so blessed. They had so much compared to many others. The work was hard and long some days, but she always had time to enjoy nature. She especially loved the river, which swiftly moved through the canyons and in her heart as well.

Carmen had dinner almost ready as Sarah entered. She turned and, seeing her daughter, her voice rang out, "Mija, you're home. I'm so glad, we will eat as soon as your father arrives."

It was close to four p.m. The red chile and frijoles filled the house with an aroma that made her mouth water as she looked forward to eating her mother's delicious food. Carmen was turning out tortillas on her round griddle, seasoned with love, as she had for so many years. They looked so good, Sarah couldn't resist one.

"Pray Dad gets out of the fields soon," Carmen continued. "I thought tonight we could can some green beans. The green chilies are ready to be roasted and put up, too. We do have our work cut out for us, Sarah."

Sarah went over to Carmen and, putting her arms around her, gave her a big warm hug. Smiling, she said, "I know, Mother, but at least we have fun doing the work. We can be thankful for that." Sarah could always find something to be thankful for in any situation. All the people in Velarde loved her for this and for her genuine goodness and kindness to them. As far as that goes, all who came to know Sarah loved her. If she did have any enemies, it was because of their envy over the love she received from others, and the love and tenderness she gave.

At that moment, Ernest came in, looking dirty and somewhat tired. As he entered, he was already saying, "Hello! Am I ever hungry and thirsty!" He bent down and kissed Carmen before he went right on to get cleaned up.

Ernest was of medium build, about five feet ten inches tall, a handsome man with tanned skin and deep-set hazel eyes. He had a mustache and was very distinguished-looking.

Carmen yelled after him. "Ernest, we thought we would put up the chilies, and hopefully, the green beans tonight."

Stopping, he looked at her and, with a grin, said, "Woman, do you ever get tired?" Then he was gone. Sarah and Carmen looked at each other and laughed heartily.

In Santa Fe, the day dragged on for Sheila. She tried to keep her mind on the article she was writing, but it was of no use. All she thought about was the young man she had literally run into.

I wonder how old he is? He looks like, maybe, he might be twenty-five, possibly twenty-eight or thirty. Her thoughts would not leave him. His arms felt so good around me, so strong. He is so good-looking, his smile made my heart pound with an excitement I'm not used to feeling. She went from one thought to another so fast that some of them mingled with each other. Sheila's heart felt as light as a feather.

Lunch came and went, and she still sat at her desk, daydreaming. I'm not hungry, so why should I eat? I'd rather just sit here, lost in my thoughts. I'm enjoying them more than food.

It was close to three-thirty when she stood up, gathering her tote bag and reaching for her purse. When she left the office, she took the time to stop and chat with a few of her co-workers.

Arriving at the La Fonda Hotel, she looked for Steve outside. Not seeing him anywhere, she entered and walked around the interior of the La Fonda, admiring the large vigas on the ceiling, the wide wood trim, and the natural stone floor. The old Mexican furnishings and the feel of the place always made her feel nostalgic.

A hand taking her by the elbow startled her back to where she was. Laughing amiably, Steve said, "Well, I've done it again. So far, each time we meet, I startle you."

They both were laughing good-naturedly over that as they entered the La Fiesta cocktail lounge. Anyone seeing them would never guess that they had just met this very morning. Sheila wished her heart would stop pounding. She hoped he couldn't feel it, as he was casually guiding her, still holding her arm.

I'm acting like a school girl, she was thinking, as Steve was seating her at a table in the corner. It seems so romantic in here. . . or am I just ready for romance?

That evening, while undressing and getting ready for bed, Sheila kept having flashbacks of their evening together. All the things they shared over a glass of wine. They had stayed at the La Fonda for an hour and a half, just talking and talking. Then they decided to go to the Pink Adobe for dinner.

Steve seemed to be so well-known in both places. People waved to him from different tables or said hello as they went by. At the Pink Adobe, the maitre'd knew him and sat them at a pleasant and intimate table for two. She couldn't believe it was after nine p.m. when they left the restaurant. Steve insisted on driving her home, as she had walked to work this morning.

He was twenty-seven years old. He was vice-president of his father's architectural firm, Reed & Reed. They did all the architectural work for hospitals, medical centers, banks, and corporate offices. Sheila did not understand all of it, but she knew Steve enjoyed it. He had a lot of enthusiasm for his work. He and his family, which included his parents and four siblings, all lived in Santa Fe. They were all born here. He told her so much about his family, his work, and his goals.

"In our firm, I do all the creative designs and drawings," he told her. "My brothers are satisfied to do all the plain blueprints and give me the intricate ones. It's very challenging, and I've had some other firms call to ask for consultation on complex designs. I find it very edifying because I enjoy my work so much."

"Steve, tell me more about you, who you are, what you want out of life, besides your work. Oh, I don't know what I want to hear, except more about you."

"I'm glad you want to know me, Sheila, because I feel an urge to tell you about myself. I'm the youngest in my family. My brothers and sisters are all married and have families of their own. I was born and raised a Catholic. I love my church and my faith and try to live it in my daily life and in my association with other people. I've never been married, and when I do marry, it will be forever. You see, I had what I call a conversion in my faith a few years ago when I made my confirmation. I was shocked at what was being taught. It was more like a sex education class than a class for learning about God and His commandments. I wanted to learn more about His call to each of us to live for Him, in whatever vocation He calls us to.

"From then on, I delved into the true teachings of Christ. I read all I could of good books and looked for priests who were sound and in union with the Holy Father in their teaching of faith and morals. This led me to work in my spare time with a pro-life group. Someday, I want to get married. I want to enjoy a loving marital union with the woman I plan to spend the rest of my life with. This union will have deep love and total commitment. That is my pledge to my future wife and children.

"So my prayer has been that God would send me someone who believes as I do and who is willing to accept the children God would send us."

Sheila was looking seriously into his eyes, listening to him as she never had to anyone else. "I hope you have not been offended that I have talked so intimately with you on our first time out together," he said. "I hope to see you again and I wanted to share with you how important to me it is to live a chaste life and be responsive to the service of God and others."

There was a pause, a comfortable pause, as Sheila lowered her eyes for a few seconds. Then, looking directly into Steve's eyes, she said, "I, too, have saved myself for marriage. That is why in the last two years, I have very rarely kept company with men. Oh, I have some men friends and we go out occasionally, but I have been praying to find the right man. My parents taught us well and they have had such a happy marriage themselves, I have wanted the same. As far as children go, I never thought about how many I would have, or about it having anything to do with God. But as you talked, I came to feel it was in His care. I'm not a Catholic, but I know about Catholicism, as many of my friends are Catholic. Along with my mother teaching me right from wrong, my friends have been an influence in my life.

"At slumber parties, we have talked about abortion, divorce, pre-marital sex and birth control. My friends must have been taught right because they had very good morals. They said much the same as what you told me now."

As she finished speaking, she could feel the blush on her face. She changed the subject abruptly and started sharing about her family. That she was going home for her birthday and about all the plans her mother was conjuring up for that celebration. She shared about Richard and Leah and how close they had always been. How something kept drawing her to New Mexico and to live in Santa Fe, even though her family did not understand. She even shared that she had been going through a hard time in the last few months, difficulties of a personal nature. Not once, however, did she mention Sarah or anything about having another sister. The wounds in her heart were still too raw to share about her identical twin sister whom she never knew.

Now, sitting before her dressing table and staring at herself in the mirror, she thought, Somewhere, someplace, there is a young woman who looks exactly like me. Looking closely at herself, she wished she had not cut her hair short. Everyone had liked her long auburn hair. How many times had she been told she had beautiful hair and eyes? In the mirror, she saw her expression change from happy to forlorn, as her thoughts had turned from Steve to Sarah.

She said out loud and emphatically, "That's enough! Be happy!" Then shutting the light off, she headed for bed and happy dreams of Steve.

Before falling asleep, she said a small prayer: "Dear God, let him be thinking of me."

Chapter 3

The month went by so fast that it was August twenty-fourth before she realized it. Sheila had been back home in Phoenix for a couple of days now. She shared with her family all about Steve and how they met. They all laughed at her story of practically falling into his arms. Sheila smiled as she remembered that day, one she would never forget.

"I wanted him to come home with me so he could meet you. He is a Catholic and some retreat or something was going on at church this week that he was involved in." As she said this, she closely watched to see if her parents reacted in any way. They were Christian people, but were not affiliated with any one church. Ever since she could remember, they would wander from one denomination to another. They would stay with one church for three or four years, then change to another, but they would attend church somewhere every Sunday.

She knew her grandparents on her father's side were Catholic. She remembered her grandmother giving her a rosary when she was five or six years old. Now she wondered what she did with it. Her grandparents had died at such an early age that she never did get to know them well. She knew that Grandpa and Grandmother Farrell had left her the trust fund. Coming back from her memories, she went on, "Then, too, he had a deadline to meet this week. He is drawing a set of blueprints for a large hospital and rehabilitation center." As they listened to her, they could see she was already deeply in love with him.

It was now just over three weeks since they first met. They had seen each other almost every day since then. Now, home in Phoenix, she felt the separation very deeply and wished Steve could be here for her birthday.

Going downstairs around seven-thirty a.m., she entered the dining room to the voices of some of the family.

"Happy Birthday to you. . . ."

She smiled as they all sang, and then they all hugged. That was the start of her birthday. The rest of the day was filled with surprises from family and friends. They went out to lunch. Hid cards in different places throughout the house. Had tea in the afternoon. Martha made her a special gift of her homemade penuche. She was pleased when Sheila made such a fuss over it.

The day went by and Steve had not called once. Every time she came home, she would ask, "Any calls?" The reply was always negative. Finally, she decided not to ask again. Someone would let her know if he called. She was sure they all knew who it was that she was hoping to hear from.

Steve had explained to her that he would not be able to come to Phoenix for her birthday. He and his father and brothers had a deadline to meet on a large project. It would take all of them, working as a team, to be able to meet it.

Sheila was disappointed and Steve, sensing this, had told her, "When you come home, I have special plans for the two of us to celebrate your birthday." She tried to coax out of him what the plans were, but stopped when she realized he was not sure himself yet. Instead of pushing the issue, she let him know she would be looking forward to being with him.

Ellen had a formal dinner for about twenty-five guests, including the family. It was planned for eight p.m. Martha was preparing Sheila's favorite meal. Pork chops and homemade dressing, homemade applesauce, mashed potatoes, and green beans. Sheila had also requested French onion soup for the first course, then a delicious green salad with a very special dressing that was a recipe of one of her uncles. To top it all off would be angel food cake with pineapple and whipped cream. It was a tradition in the family for each of the children, all through the years, to pick their birthday dinner. They had always enjoyed this and still held their mother to keeping this tradition. There had been a lot of joking all day long that Sheila wanted three meals in one.

As Sheila dressed for dinner, she tried to put Steve out of her mind. She was sorry he had not called her. She had hoped that he would, and she had herself all ready for his call each time the phone

She stopped and looked at her mother, who was still holding her hand and looking at her intently.

"Mother, we're not going to do anything foolish. We have only known each other a short time, but we have shared very intimately about our convictions. We both have parents that have given us principles and values to live by. Mom, I'm very thankful to you and Dad for the good Christian beliefs that you have passed on to your children. Steve is very mature. I know we still have a lot to learn about each other, and I'm sure the families will meet.

"As far as our family and learning about Sarah, I feel that I have handled everything that has happened very well. I'm not in some kind of depression over it. In fact, I feel that I have done well in taking a situation that is beyond my control and dealing with it. I think we have all done so, Mother.

"If it makes you feel any better, neither one of us wants to rush into marriage. You all will know Steve and his family, and so shall I, before any announcement of an engagement. He hasn't asked me to marry him. As you said yourself, we have only known each other a few weeks." Then she surprised herself by saying, "However, Mother, I know that Steve is the man I will marry someday!"

They sat in silence for a few moments, sipping their tea, before Ellen had the courage to ask her, "Why have you not told him about Sarah?"

Sheila took a deep breath. "I will, when I can talk about it. When the time comes, I'll know. It took me twenty-one years to learn of her. I'm not ready yet to share her with anyone, but when I am ready, Steve will be the first one I share with."

They hugged each other tenderly before Ellen left the room. Both women lay awake, each engrossed in her own personal thoughts, before falling asleep.

By September thirtieth, Sheila was caught up in her regular routine. She was back in Santa Fe by the end of August. She and Steve had been seeing each other every day. Work was going smoothly, and she was more contented than she had been in a long time.

She liked Steve's family very much. Mary, his mother, was a warm and friendly woman, tall and slightly heavy, stylish yet simple. Now that her children were raised and Steve was the only one still living at home, she worked at the office everyday with her husband. Being a very competent business woman, her husband and sons were happy to have her there. Two other women helped her but she did the main secretarial work for the firm. She enjoyed it very much.

Jim, his father, was a very distinguished man, tall, and his smile was broad showing the laugh lines around his eyes. He had a dry sense of humor which the family delighted in. Steve looked like his father and still had the warm simple way of his mother.

Sheila hoped to have the families meet very soon. Still, she wanted to hold them off a little longer. She still had not told Steve about Sarah, although she was planning to, soon.

Little did she know that, on this day, her twin sister was opening her eyes in Velarde, New Mexico, wondering what her mother had planned for her birthday.

Chapter 4

It was September thirtieth and Sarah woke early, thinking about her birthday. Although she knew that this was actually the day she was given to her parents by her birth mother, she still thought of it as her birthday. She dressed quickly. As the sun was coming up, she was already out walking along the river that ran in back of her home. She could see the house in the distance.

Walking along at a pretty good pace, she watched the river as it moved rapidly. Her own thoughts were moving right along, too. Every birthday, she thought about who she really was. Her real parents, what were they like? She wondered if her father was still alive and, if he was, did he still live in Phoenix, Arizona?

As far as Sarah was concerned, Carmen and Ernest would always be her parents. She loved them dearly and thanked God for them every day. They never adopted her, but they loved and raised her as their very own, ever since she was given to them by her mother. Now, as she walked along, she once again remembered parts of what they had told her when she was fourteen years old. They never adopted her, as Laura gave her to them as if she were their very own. They had no money for court fees or whatever the state would want and, being simple people, they felt it best.

Then, when Laura died so suddenly after leaving her daughter with them and making them solemnly promise to keep her and not tell her parents, they went through a lot of suffering as to what they should do. They decided not to do anything. Laura's father was an alcoholic who abused his wife and children. They loved Sarah and did not want her to be thrust into that kind of life.

How hard it was for her to believe when they explained that she was not their real daughter. It had been a shock; she could not believe it at first. It was hard for Carmen and Ernest to tell her because they felt as though she was their very own flesh and blood from the first moment she came into their lives. Sarah remembered vividly the facts they had told her.

Carmen had lost their only child three months before, at birth. She was told she could never have anymore children, and was heartbroken. Ernest had a distant relative who lived in Phoenix, Arizona. She had a daughter named Laura. They rarely saw these relatives because of the distance between them. Occasionally, throughout the years, they would see each other at weddings and funerals.

Carmen had told Sarah she never would forget the day—September thirtieth—when a rap came at their door in the late afternoon. Ernest, upon opening the door, was surprised to see a frightened young girl, holding a tiny infant. Laura had teased hair that looked dirty the way it stuck up in the air. She wore jeans and a tight blouse. She was short, but thin. A pretty girl; wearing so much makeup it hid how pretty she was. Her lips were red and outlined with a dark black-red.

At first, he did not recognize her. She told him who she was. They welcomed her into their home and Carmen asked if she was hungry. When she said she was, Carmen went right to work, making her some hot tea, and a steaming bowl of chili colorado and tortillas.

Laura had put the baby on the sofa. Carmen could not take her eyes off the tiny little girl. Carmen and Ernest asked no questions as Laura ate her dinner. Nor did they have to wait long for her story to come out.

A tearful Laura told them she had a baby out of wedlock. Her mother and father knew nothing about it. She wanted them to promise her they would never tell any of the family. She told them her boyfriend threatened to leave her if she did not give the baby away.

She was only seventeen and she could not support herself and a baby. She was frantic and thought of them, of the beautiful, peaceful valley they lived in, far away from Phoenix. She remembered she had heard recently that Carmen had lost her baby. She came here to Velarde, to beg them to take her little girl. No questions asked. They must promise never to tell her family. It was the only condition she had and she kept insisting upon it. She broke down into exhausted tears and Carmen tried to comfort her the best she could.

After Laura and little Sarah were settled in bed, Ernest and Carmen stayed up most of the night praying and talking about what they should do. Carmen wanted the baby desperately. She was part of Ernest's family; why couldn't they raise her as their own?

Ernest was reticent, but finally gave in. He wanted little Sarah as much as Carmen did. So, it was final. They would keep the baby.

Sarah was Anglo. They thought nothing of this as Laura did not look Hispanic. Her mother had married an Anglo and they did not know her boyfriend's nationality. Laura stayed with them for two days and they did nothing but pray and talk. The girl was so hysterical. She told them she wanted a good loving home for the baby. She couldn't take her home. "I don't ever want my parents to know about her. It is hell in our house. She wouldn't have a good home. Promise me, promise you will raise her and never take her back to Phoenix or tell my parents. I never want them to know."

Carmen talked to Laura about breaking away from this boyfriend. She told her she should go to confession and she offered for Laura to stay and live with her and Ernest and little Sarah. Laura thanked them and said she would think about all that Carmen told her.

It was several months before they heard, through Carmen's sister in Santa Fe, the news that Laura had been killed in an automobile accident in Phoenix. She was with some young people, a few of whom were drinking. They had left a party about two a.m. and their speeding car crashed into a large tree on a bend in the road. Laura was killed instantly. It had been only two and a half weeks since the day she had left Sarah with them.

Laura had told them she named her baby Sarah. That she was a little over a month old. They did not know her exact birthday, so they chose September thirtieth, as that was the day she came to them. A month would not matter that much, they reasoned. She had not given them the name of her boyfriend, Sarah's supposed father. "He knows nothing of my bringing you the baby," Laura had said. "I borrowed a car and have been driving for hours to get here. I never want him to know where she is."

Sarah thought of all these things as she walked along the Rio Grande. She was so happy being with Ernest and Carmen and loved them dearly as her very own parents. She knew they felt the same about her being their own daughter.

Sometimes, though, she felt a void in her life, an emptiness or loneliness for someone or something. At times she felt a part of her was missing; she couldn't explain it. . . . this deep inner feeling of abandonment.

It was almost seven a.m. as she neared Iglesia de La Virgen de Guadalupe (Our Lady of Guadalupe Church). Mass would be starting soon. Sarah was baptized in this church only a few weeks after arriving in Velarde. She greeted Father Joseph, then entered the church. Kneeling in silent prayer, she gave thanks to God and to His holy Mother. She prayed for her family and friends, for the world and all people. She asked God's blessings for everyone.

The small community of daily church-goers greeted her after Mass with happy wishes for her birthday. They talked for a few minutes before Sarah started walking home. One of her friends accompanied her part of the way. Sarah loved the people here; they were simple, yet refined. They were a sensitive people who were always there to help each other.

Carmen and Ernest were eagerly waiting to have breakfast with her when she got home. She could smell the aroma of bacon and coffee drifting out the door and window, and she picked up her gait as she realized she was hungry and anxious to see her parents.

At breakfast, she told them the news they had been waiting for. "Dad and Mom, I received a birthday letter from Mother Mary Gabriel. She said that next weekend would be a difficult time to see us. She asked us to come to Santa Fe on Saturday, October twelfth. She could have a private visit with me in the morning and then a short visit with all of us."

Carmen looked at her daughter lovingly. "Mija, if everything goes as planned, you will be entering the Carmelite monastery so soon. We have so much to prepare. Do you think Mother Mary Gabriel will give you a date when you see her in October?"

Sarah replied wistfully, "I hope so, Mother. As far as I know, it will be sometime in January. It does not seem possible that, God willing, in three months or so, I will be entering the monastery. Mother Mary Gabriel wants me to be home with you for Christmas. She said Christmas is a hard time to enter the convent." Sarah hesitated for a moment and looked at Ernest, who was still sitting at the table, enjoying his coffee while listening to them as they talked. She took a deep breath before going on. "I wanted to tell you both that on my last visit, I told Mother Mary Gabriel you were not my real parents."

At this, Carmen's eyes filled up with tears. Sarah went to her and, embracing her, said quietly, "Mother, don't cry. You know as far as I am concerned, you are and always will be my parents. Still, if I'm going to be able to enter the convent, I must tell all I know about myself."

Carmen hugged her daughter, and with a slight laugh, now said, "Mija, I liked it better when you were a little girl and I watched you play and sing and dance in the wide, open spaces here. Now you will be leaving us so soon," she cried. "And I'm missing you already."

Ernest came over to them both. "Let me in on this hug." He smiled. "I have a surprise for both of you. We're going out to dinner tonight, in Taos, to celebrate your birthday, Sarah."

"Dad!" Sarah exclaimed. "Can we afford it?"

"No," he replied bluntly. "But it's my little girl's twenty-second birthday. To surprise you and your mother, I have been putting away a few dollars here and there. So, we're going. That's all there is to it." He was smiling broadly now, as he received pleasure from their happiness and excitement.

Sarah turned to Carmen. "Mother, I'll wear that new green dress you made for me."

The day went swiftly by. There were so many daily tasks, heavy and light, that needed to be done on a farm. Sarah's heart sang all day with happiness. She bubbled with excitement and anticipation about going to Taos. This would be a wonderful birthday. The three of them enjoyed doing things together and Carmen would not have to cook. She knew how much her mother enjoyed going out to dinner. Sarah had worked one summer as a waitress at Michael's and had enjoyed it so much. It was a Mexican restaurant and bakery in Taos.

They arrived in Taos early in the afternoon so the two women could do some shopping. Dinner at Michael's was exceptionally good. They were all in a festive mood. Sarah knew quite a few of the old staff. They came by their table, wishing her birthday blessings and congratulations.

During dinner, Sarah came back to their earlier conversation of entering the convent. "I believe I finally have chosen the name I will take when entering." She looked radiant as she spoke and shared this decision with her family. "I chose Sister Michael Raphael." Sarah waited for their approval; she received it from their warm smiles and the words that followed. Their response let her know they, too, liked the name she would use the rest of her life in the convent. Sister Michael Raphael of the Holy Angels. "You know St. Michael the Archangel has always been my beloved patron. I think it is most appropriate that I chose his name."

Sarah had been trying to choose the right name ever since she decided she would become a nun. Ernest and Carmen would suggest some, on and off, but none of them seemed right until now. She was pleased that on this birthday, she had finally decided and her parents were in agreement. She would tell Mother Mary Gabriel on October twelfth.

On the way home, they sang, talked, laughed, and gave thanks to God.

Once in bed, Sarah could not get to sleep. Memories of Carmel kept flashing back to her.

Whenever they went to Santa Fe and visited her aunt, they went to church in the small chapel at Carmel. She loved it and could remember how timid and wide-eyed she was with the extern sister who was so nice to her. The first time she could remember Carmel, she was only five or six years old. She loved Mass and hearing and knowing about Jesus and Mary. It wasn't until the tragic accident that left her almost dead, when she was eleven, that she felt called to enter Carmel.

As she lay awake, she pictured the parlor where you would visit Mother and the other sisters. This would be where her family and friends would visit her after she entered. The first time she saw the iron bars of the grille in the parlor, they looked enormous. The grille itself never scared her, though; the love of the sisters made the grille seem insignificant. She remembered visiting the nuns with her parents. They would be on one side of the grille and the nuns on the other side of the bars. When the sisters took their leave, they would draw the curtain across the bars.

As a little girl, Sarah loved the Carmelite order and now she was so happy she was almost part of it. She pictured herself in the long brown habit with Mary's mantle, the scapular over her shoulders, and the cord and rosary around her waist.

There was a smile on her face as she finally fell asleep.

Chapter 5

October twelfth was fast approaching. Ernest and Carmen talked about how they would be able to make this trip to Santa Fe with Sarah. Money was tight. They were helping Sarah purchase the items on the list that Mother Mary Gabriel had given her on her last visit. Material for her brown wool habit. A set of sheets, towels, pillow cases, jacket, boots, and other necessities. All the different articles a new novice would bring when she entered the convent. They both trusted that somehow God would provide for this trip. They needed to be together for these special events leading up to their daughter's entrance into Carmel.

She would be a cloistered nun in perpetual solitude. They would never be able to physically hug her once she entered. How could they explain to their family and friends their happiness and thanksgiving to God for calling Sarah into the Order of the Blessed Virgin Mary of Mt. Carmel?

Some of the family could not understand the idea of putting yourself into a cloistered order. They thought that the Carmelites did no work and couldn't understand what their purpose was. As much as Carmen would try to explain, she would always fall short of getting her message out the right way. Sometimes, she would get so frustrated over this; she would carry on in private to Ernest about it all.

Ernest would sit and listen patiently, then tell her not to worry, or care, who understood or who did not. He would remind her that what mattered was to live one day at a time for God and His Mother and to be thankful for all the graces they receive.

Sarah, too, had so much to think about. How could she help her parents out? They were so good to her, so faithful to God. She thanked God so many times for their devout faith and that He had brought her to them, and to Him through them.

They trusted always, no matter what the circumstances. Sarah had so much respect for them and loved them dearly. Now, though, she was going through an inner conflict. She knew they were troubled over finances and they wanted so much for everything to be perfect for her. She needed to help them.

One day when she and Carmen were preparing dinner, she brought the subject up. "Mother, I know you and Dad are concerned about the trip to Santa Fe and all the expense coming up right now. . . ."

Carmen interrupted. "Mija, I'm so sorry that you have seen this. We do not want you to worry. God will provide."

Sighing, because she knew her parents were not going to like what she was about to do, Sarah proceeded, "Mother, listen to me. I am going back to work at Michael's."

Carmen put her hands up. "No, my daughter, that is not necessary."

Knowing that it was necessary and that it would help them immensely, Sarah continued. "I have almost three months I can work before I enter the convent. Angela drives to Taos every day. We have worked it out so I can ride with her. Don't say anything, Mama, just listen to me. John has already rehired me. He said I was a good waitress and they would be happy to let me work, even though it is only for a short time. I believe it is God's holy will, since all the doors have been opened for me." And she added happily, "The best thing is, I can start now, and John said they would let me off for the three days we need to go to Santa Fe."

Carmen, who had tried several times to get a word in, finally interjected, "No, mija, we do not like it. It is too much for you. It was hard before, when you went so far to work and still did so much work here on the farm. You help Dad and me so much right here, my little mija."

Sarah was firm. "Mother, I've prayed about this. I'm going to do it. I told John I would start tomorrow. Angela is picking me up at seven a.m. Everything has worked out so that I know in my heart God has confirmed this decision. It will take the pressure off of you and Dad. We will be able to have some money to purchase what I need for Carmel and for our trip to visit Mother Mary Gabriel. We can do some of the things we have always wanted to do." Sarah stopped cutting the onions. She put her arms around Carmen and hugged her tightly. "How can I ever thank you and Dad for all you have done for me? I have always been so very happy here. You gave me my faith, brought me up to love the Church and the sacraments. You have taught me to love God and His Holy Mother, the angels and saints. You have given me the best that any parent could give to a child. I will miss being with you both so much. My memories of this valley and farmland, the river that I love, the gorges and canyons and the people here will always live in my heart.

"I love you all, Mama, but still my heart is calling me to Carmel with great anticipation. When I enter, you will all go with me in spirit and you will always be with me—a part of me."

By now, both women were crying and holding each other. Sarah was the first to pull herself away. Looking earnestly into Carmen's eyes, she said, "Promise to help me tell Dad my plans about working. It is the only way we can do the things we want to do."

Carmen nodded to her daughter's plea. She knew Ernest would not approve, but she would smooth it over somehow. After all, Sarah had enjoyed working before. She got away from the farm for a little while and would have some time to be with friends. It could be good for her at this time. Carmen dried her eyes as she spoke. "Why don't you run out to church and see Father Joseph? He has been your spiritual director for the past few years. It will help if I can tell your Dad that Father Joseph agrees with you."

Sarah's eyes lit up. "I'll go by the river so I can pray and read for a little while. I have been wanting to finish my book. Then I'll go see Father and be back for dinner." She kissed her mother on the cheek, grabbed her shawl and book and was out the door in a flash.

Carmen went to the door and watched as Sarah started to run and sing at the same time.

Oh, what a blessing this child has been, she thought. She couldn't help feeling happy and sad at the same time.

The last thing she saw before turning to go back to her cooking was Ernest, walking up through the fields. He was looking toward Sarah, whom he could not hear, but could still see, faintly, in the distance.

In Santa Fe, all was going well between Steve and Sheila. They were dating regularly. Sheila was impressed with his family. She felt like she had always known Jim and Mary Reed and Steve's brothers and sisters. It would be easy for her to adjust to calling Mary "Mom". She knew they liked her and were already hoping she would be their daughter-in-law.

Last week, she and Steve went to church together. Sheila was a little in awe when he took her to Mass at St. Francis Cathedral. As she sat and watched him go up to receive Holy Communion, she couldn't help thinking that he would be a good husband and father. He was not ashamed to be reverent, to be in prayer with his hands folded upright as he walked up the aisle. Her friends had told her about communion and believing it was Jesus. It was obvious that Steve knew Jesus was truly present in the Holy Eucharist. A man who is strong enough to live for God and confident enough not to care what others think would always be faithful to his wife. He would be good to her and to their children, Sheila thought.

Steve's parents were at church and the four of them went to La Fonda for breakfast after Mass. Plans were made for Sheila's family to be invited for dinner at the Reed's on October twenty-eighth. Sheila told them she would call her parents right away, since the twenty-eighth was a little less than two weeks away.

When Ellen received the call from Sheila, she made it perfectly clear that it was about time they met Steve and his family. Howard and Ellen would plan on staying with Sheila for a few days. She would tell the rest of the family and see if they would be able to come for a couple of days.

Before they finished talking, Ellen asked once again if Steve knew about Sarah. She was obviously disappointed that Sheila had not told him yet. She asked Ellen not to mention anything to him or his family until she was ready to do so herself. Ellen reluctantly made this promise to her daughter.

It was only a few more days before Sheila's family would be in Santa Fe. Steve and Sheila were out to dinner. They were enjoying themselves, talking about so many different things, their families, beliefs, Santa Fe, recreation. Sheila was happy they had so many of the same interests.

After some thought, Sheila decided it was time to broach another subject. "Steve, we have shared intimately about so many things such as faith, marriage, children, and work, but we have never talked about money or finances. I know you have a good job that you love. . . ."

"Sheila, I should have thought of this myself. I make a good annual salary. Our firm has an investment plan and I have about seventeen thousand dollars built up in that at this time. At my age, I think I am pretty well established. I try to put something away for retirement. I live well now, but I'm not interested in money. I could have a lot more, but I try to help a pro-life group with the extra money."

Before he could go on any further, Sheila broke in, "I did not mean to get so personal about your finances until you were ready to tell me. I don't know why I mentioned your work. You see, I brought this subject up because I needed to tell you more about me. My grandparents have left me a large sum of money. . . at this time I have well over a million and a half dollars." She watched him closely. Utter silence followed her statement. Steve was at a loss for words.

"It doesn't make any difference to you, does it, Steve? I'm still the same. I'm not any different whether I have money or not." After a pause, "Answer me, Steve. Does it make any difference to you?" She found herself getting anxious as she looked at him. He was ashen and blank.

Most men wanted her money; now here she was worried over losing the one she loved because of it.

Finally, he regained his composure. "Sheila, I knew you lived well and had your own house, but to tell the truth, I did not think that much about it. I thought your family was helping you." He added feebly, "I guess I never even thought about money until you brought it up. Does it mean a lot to you. . . having so much wealth?"

"No. No. . . I don't know. I enjoy being able to do whatever I want and have whatever I desire. Steve, how do you feel about it?"

"I have to think about it, Sheila. I need to know, do you find ways to help others or do you keep it all for yourself? What I'm trying to say is, it's not wrong to live comfortably and fulfill your needs and some of your desires, but then we need to help others."

"I did not receive the money until I was twenty-one. Only a short time ago. I haven't thought about helping anyone. I know my mother and father give to different charities, but I never paid much attention. I've always had everything I've ever wanted. I've never thought much about people being in need."

"Sheila, I do not want a lot of money. I've noticed the more money people have, the more they seem to worry about losing it or doubling it. Not everyone, but some get selfish and try to find ways to get more and more. As I said, it is not wrong to enjoy life and live well, but my beliefs take me a different way. Somewhere in the scriptures it says, 'they used what they needed and gave the rest to help the poor'. That does not mean they did not take care of themselves. They did, but they set their sights on a higher goal—life everlasting."

Now it was Sheila who looked bewildered and helpless. She never thought of such things. She wished she had not brought the subject up and was very uneasy. She had not anticipated this kind of a reaction and was on the verge of tears. They ate in silence for a few moments that seemed like an eternity.

Steve reached for her hand. As she looked up, he was smiling at her and his smile made her heart quiver. "Come on, now, don't look so sad and forlorn. What's a little money? I'm sure there is a way to find out how to use some and dispose of the rest."

The tension was broken, and they both laughed. "Don't worry, Sheila. To answer your question, I don't care if you have money or not. I love you. If we decide to marry, we would have to talk a lot more about this, but I'm sure God would help us know what to do. We only have to trust in Him." Sheila breathed a sigh of relief. She loved him too much to lose him over money. Who ever would have thought she'd have that problem? Steve always amazed her with his deep feelings and convictions.

They were halfway through their meal when Sheila almost choked on her food. Steve was once again looking at her intently and saying, "Sheila, why is it that you look so much like someone I should know, or think I know?"

Putting her napkin to her mouth and swallowing hard, she exclaimed, "You said that once before!" Even as she spoke, her mind was flashing back to the first time they met and Steve saying, "I'm sorry that I held you like that, but for a moment, I thought I recognized you."

At the time, his remark had not registered at all, but now, as he said this and the way he was looking at her, she was filled with anticipation.

"Steve, what do you mean? Who do I resemble? Where is she? How long have you known her?" Sheila's excitement was growing as she spoke. She was gripping the table and leaning toward Steve. Her knuckles were white.

Steve was deeply concerned when he saw how agitated she was. He reached over and put his hand on hers; they were ice cold.

"Sheila, slow down. Try to get ahold of yourself. You are so pale, you look like you are going to faint."

Sheila sat in silence as he paid the check. He could see she was deeply troubled as painful emotions would express themselves, first in her eyes and then, on her face. Leaving the restaurant, Sheila finally spoke. "Steve, come to the house. We need to talk. There is something I have not told you. Now is the time."

As they sat on the couch and held hands, Sheila told him about Sarah. . . everything, from the moment she first received the letter from the bank that referred to Sarah and the trust fund. About her different trips in search of her sister. How, on this last trip, she was so heart-broken when she faced the woman who she thought might be her sister, only to find out that she was not. Finally, how she was trying, unsuccessfully, to put Sarah out of her thoughts.

When she had finished, Steve, who had been listening intently, asked, "Why have you not told me this sooner?" She could feel his strength as he warmly held her hands.

With tears in her eyes, she simply said, "It was too hard."

They talked for a very long time. He left her well after two a.m. Sheila felt better now that she finally knew about her twin sister. She felt comforted as he held her and kissed her gently before leaving. This had been an exhausting night, telling Steve about her wealth, being stunned by his reaction, and then telling him all about Sarah.

Sheila had hopes in the restaurant that Steve knew who it was she resembled. She felt great disappointment as he revealed to her he did not actually know anyone. He thought, now more than ever, that he had either met or had seen someone, someplace that looked just like her. Sheila tried to probe his memory all night. She asked him so many questions.

"Steve, this is so important. Try to remember, please. Could it be someone you do business with? Or maybe someone you saw at a business lunch or at a meeting? What about the group you work with? Does she help out there?"

"Sheila, I've racked my brains. I know I have seen someone, someplace that looks like you, but I do not know who or where. I'm so sorry."

As they talked well into the night, Steve told her that in the back of his mind, he would feel he almost had it. Then—nothing; he would go blank.

Before he left, he assured her he would keep trying to remember and he would help her find Sarah if she was still alive.

Now as she lay awake, she felt a cold chill. Steve had said they would find her "if she were still alive". The thought had never occurred to her that Sarah might be dead. She shuddered and prayed. "Oh, God, let her be alive, let us find her."

Howard and Ellen had told her the authorities believed Sarah was probably still in the Phoenix area. Or somewhere in Arizona, possibly California. Sheila's thoughts kept racing. Maybe that is why no one responded to the picture in the paper. The detective agency she had hired had put her picture in the newspapers, requesting any information from anyone who might know this woman. There was no response. If Sarah were dead. . . .

Now her teeth were chattering as she lay there in the still and quiet of the morning with Steve's words going through her mind: "We will find her, if she is still alive. We will do it together!"

Steve called Sheila first thing in the morning. She was up and waiting for his call. Grasping the phone tightly, she told him, "Steve, please do not say anything to my parents when they come. We will tell your parents about Sarah after they leave. I do not want to get their hopes up once again. I have done that too many times in the last few months. I will tell my mother that I told you I have a twin sister. That will relieve her mind for now." Then she continued in anguish, "Steve, what if you can't remember where you saw her, or," She paused briefly and her voice shook as she finished the sentence.

"Maybe she is dead?"

Chapter 6

Sheila could not believe it was early December already. So much had happened in the last few weeks. The Reeds and the Farrells met at dinner back in October at the Reeds' home.

Howard, Ellen, and Leah had spent a week with Sheila. Ellen was anxious to meet Jim and Mary Reed and their family.

The day of the dinner party, Ellen had her hair done. Sheila and Leah couldn't help but laugh at how she was acting over meeting Steve's family.

"Mother," Leah said. "Why can't you relax? You'd think you were unaccustomed to meeting new people or going out to dinner."

Sheila chimed in, "I've told you over and over how much you're going to like them. Mary is so natural and she is a great cook."

Ellen made a face at the two of them, causing them to laugh all the harder. "Leave me alone, both of you. If I want to fuss a little, then let me do it. Besides, Sheila, if you do marry Steve, I want to like his family and I want them to feel the same about us. Is that so funny?" She paused. "Well, all I know is, I'll feel better once we do meet."

Howard came into the room and picked up Ellen's words. "You won't have to wait long, my dear. Shouldn't we be leaving in the next few minutes?"

All eyes turned toward him. "Dad, you look great," Sheila said, as she jumped up and grabbed his hands and they twirled around the room. Sheila couldn't hide her excitement, and Ellen and Leah smiled at each other.

Ellen's worries proved needless; the families hit it off immediately. Dinner was splendid. Jim grilled fresh salmon. The men stood

45

outside with him and talked as he cooked. Mary made a broccoli souffle, with garlic oven potatoes, a fruit salad, and homemade dinner rolls. For dessert, she had a pie made with cream cheese on the bottom crust and fluffy pumpkin on the top, with a dollop of cream. It was delicious.

Sheila was pleased with the evening. Steve couldn't seem to take his eyes off of her. She found herself loving him more than ever.

The next month, Sheila, Steve, and his parents drove to the Farrell's home in Phoenix for Thanksgiving dinner. They arrived on Wednesday evening and left Sunday morning and all agreed it was a wonderful weekend.

Steve and his parents went to church Thanksgiving morning, and asked Sheila, Howard, and Ellen to accompany them. Sheila was delighted. She had been to Mass several times with Steve. Her parents hesitated, but then decided to join them.

When they arrived home after church, the aroma of the turkey filled the house. Dinner was delicious, as always. Martha made dressing with rich creamy gravy, mashed potatoes topped with butter that slowly melted, green peas, small pearl buttered onions, corn casserole, sweet potatoes, homemade cranberry-orange relish, and rolls. Everyone loved the desserts. Ellen and Leah had spent two weeks before Thanksgiving helping Martha bake pies, Christmas cookies, pumpkin rolls, nut balls, and Martha's famous penuche fudge.

Ellen enjoyed this family time. She and Martha and the children had baked together for many years. Martha was an excellent cook and there was no need for them to do any cooking or baking. It was an unwritten law, though, that Ellen and the children would help her bake for the two weeks before Thanksgiving. Richard was always included as they were growing up and he enjoyed it as much as the girls did. Martha loved it. She had lived with the Farrells for over thirty years and she felt like family. They felt the same way about her.

Preparations for Thanksgiving and Christmas was a tradition they loved. Ellen knew that these memories would remain with her children forever. This year, Sue brought Cynthia and Lisa over so they could help Martha and start enjoying this holiday tradition. All through the years, they made plenty of nut balls. They were great right out of the freezer and many hands delighted in snitching and munching on them all through the Christmas season. Sheila had so many fond memories of these times together. She would always remember how they laughed at each other being caught snitching the nut balls and munching on them. Martha would pretend to reprimand them, saying, "There won't be any left for Christmas with you all taking them out of the freezer." Then Martha would act sheepish when she got caught. Sheila smiled thinking about it now.

The only drawback in Sheila's life was her missing sister. Steve had spent many days and nights trying to remember where he could have seen her, but to no avail. He could not understand why he felt so strongly about it, when evidently, this woman was no one he actually knew. If Sheila's sister was an acquaintance, he was sure he would remember her. How could he ever forget someone like Sheila? He was happy that she told him about her sister, but he wished his memory of this other woman had not raised so much hope in her.

It was raining out and overcast. Sheila had a pleasant warmth within her despite the weather as she waited outside the Gazette, under the covered entrance, for Steve to pick her up for lunch. It was chilly, but it was the kind of weather she loved. The smell, the feel, the look of the rain was uplifting.

As Steve stopped in front, she ran over and slid into the front seat. Laughing, she said, "Isn't this great? Let's eat where we can look out at the rain. I like to eat at a restaurant when it is raining and sit next to a window so I can enjoy it."

They went to the Bishop's Lodge and were able to get a table on the enclosed porch. It was so pleasant. From their table, they had a view of the grounds. The rain falling steadily through the trees made everything look exceptionally appealing.

They were deeply engrossed in conversation when a large hand slapped Steve on the shoulder.

Gary, a long time friend of his, was saying, "So you did meet her after all, and you never told me."

Stunned, both of them stared at him until, finally, he said, "What's wrong?"

Standing up and shaking hands, Steve introduced Sheila. His mind, however, remembered where he had seen Sarah before. As soon as Gary had uttered those words, he remembered. They were on a skiing trip in Taos and had stopped to have dinner. A waitress there had caught his attention. He had told Gary at the time, "Now there is a girl I would like to meet."

He had meant it, but they left and he never saw her again. That had been last winter. When Sheila stumbled into him, on the street, back in August, it triggered his memory slightly, but not enough to remember where he had seen her.

As he stood talking to Gary, he could see that Sheila was growing anxious. She knew he remembered. He reached over and put his hand on hers. Looking right into her eyes, he gave her an "I know" squeeze. He did not ask Gary to sit down. After talking briefly, his friend got the idea and excused himself with a brief "Nice to meet you" to Sheila. He left as quickly as he had come.

Steve sat down and both their hands clasped. "Sheila, I know it was in Taos last winter. She was a waitress in a restaurant there. She did not wait on us, but I told my friend, Gary, I would like to meet her. It was so brief. She had impressed me as being a very nice young lady whom I could easily be interested in. I forgot it outwardly, but my subconscious remembered. When I held you for an instant that day, I knew I wanted to meet you and not let it be just a passing encounter."

Sheila had been listening with all her heart and holding his hand tightly. Now she said, "Steve, we need to go to Taos tomorrow. We must go to that restaurant. Please, say we will go together. We will find her, I know we will! I feel it so strongly."

They made plans to leave early the next morning. Steve checked the date on his watch. Tomorrow would be Thursday, December fourteenth. He would have to reschedule some appointments. He could not let Sheila down. She needed him and she was more important to him than anyone else.

All night, Sheila tossed and turned. She would wake up and not be able to go back to sleep for two or three hours. She had been to Taos so many times. Ever since she was a small child, she had gone there with her family. Could it be possible that her sister lived in Taos, New Mexico all this time?

Steve told her that it was at Michael's Restaurant where he had seen the woman who resembled her, who he now felt sure was her sister, Sarah.

What if she is not working there anymore? How will I approach her when I see her? What if it isn't my sister? These thoughts and many more kept waking her up.

At eight a.m., she was ready to leave. Steve was right on time. He had picked up some coffee and bagels for them to eat on the way. As they drove along the Taos highway with all its twists and turns, so did their minds seem to twist one way, then another, with ideas of what they would do.

At one point, Steve said, "You can't walk in the restaurant the way you look. What if she does not know she had a twin sister? The shock of you walking in and coming face to face with her might frighten her. It is not a good idea. Maybe I should go in and see if she is there. If she isn't, I will ask some questions." He stopped and was deep in thought before he went on. "Maybe we should contact the police or the detective agency you hired."

Sheila interrupted briskly. "No, if we find her and she really is my very own sister, I don't want the police involved. Let us ask her about her life or what she knows about who she is." She looked at him now with such apprehension. "Oh, Steve, what if we don't find her?" He reached over and took her hand. They sat in silence for several minutes until Taos loomed ahead of them. Sheila looked at her watch. It was close to nine-fifteen. Already, the street was busy with cars and pedestrians.

"Steve, you're right. I can't just walk into that restaurant. Stop at Wal-Mart. I'll pick up a hat, a hair clip, a scarf and some large dark sunglasses. I can pull my hair up and hide it and the sunglasses should do the trick of hiding my face."

They were carrying the bags with all the items Sheila had purchased to disguise herself. As they reached the car, someone yelled over to her, "Sarah, where did you get that outfit? You look beautiful!"

Sheila went ashen and gripped the door handle. Steve put his arm around her to support her as they both looked at the girl who had called to them. She kept walking toward Wal-Mart, but was looking back with her hand up over her eyes squinting at them and smiling. Sheila whispered, "Shall we go after her? Should we ask her where Sarah is?" She was pulling on his arm. "What should we do?"

Steve did not know what to do, but on impulse he said, "We know now that it is Sarah. Let's go to Michael's. If we don't find her ourselves, we will have to bring in the authorities." Steve was pretty shaken up himself from hearing that girl call out Sarah's name, so he could empathize with Sheila's apprehension.

As soon as they got in the car, he tried to reassure her. "If we are going to be able to carry on with this investigation, we will have to pull ourselves together. Do you think you can do it? Can you go into Michael's and, if you see her, hold yourself together until we decide what to do? Are you strong enough to go through with this?"

Sheila, looking directly at him as he parked across from the restaurant, replied, "I am a strong person. Even though I'm shook up and feel this awful inner turmoil, I know, with you beside me, I can go through anything."

He smiled, took her hands in his, bent over and kissed her. They looked lovingly at each other for a moment. Then, with determination, they got out of the car and crossed the street toward the restaurant.

As they were walking, Sheila put the sunglasses on, which completed the disguise she had been putting on while in the car. Michael's was full. They put their name on the waiting list and stood as far out of the way as possible. They looked around at the people who worked there. They could not really see into the main part of the restaurant, and only once or twice saw a waitress go by.

Sheila had her head lowered and was gripping Steve's hand the entire time they waited. Finally, at the table, she tried to loosen up a little. She was so tense, her face felt frozen and taut.

They were at a round booth and sat so that they had a good view of the room they were in. When their waitress came to the table, Sheila kept her head down, looking at the menu, as Steve ordered for them both. Her scarf was wrapped loosely around her neck, her hat pulled low on her forehead with not a trace of hair showing, and sunglasses were still on.

They were sipping their coffee when they both saw Sarah at the same time. Steve had his arm around Sheila and held her as close to him as he could. Her body was trembling. They both watched Sarah delivering breakfast plates to the table directly across from them.

Sheila was fascinated as she watched. It was like seeing herself in another person. Sarah had the most pleasant manner, and a happy and serene look. She seemed to know the people at the table and bantered with them as she put the plates down. She spoke Spanish to some of them. She returned immediately to refill their coffee, then turned and looking directly at Steve and Sheila, asked pleasantly, "Would you like a refill?"

Sheila had to gulp many times to control the lump in her throat and the cry that wanted to escape her lips. She felt she had been holding her breath the entire time. All these emotions were so formidable, she had to fight with all her strength to control them. Steve must have felt strong emotions, too, because he only nodded that they would take more coffee. After she filled their cups and left the table, Sheila whispered, "She even sounds like I do. We are different in our manners and the way we talk, yet we are physically identical."

They only picked at their food. They took every opportunity to watch Sarah as she waited on her tables. They spoke quietly to each other about the bizarre circumstances and what their next move should be.

Sheila could hardly talk; her throat kept constricting as she fought to keep from sobbing. She wanted to jump up and grab Sarah and say, "You're my sister!"

They left the restaurant about eleven forty-five. It was too conspicuous for them to stay any longer.

When Steve paid, he asked the name of the waitress with the auburn hair. "Sarah Montoya" he was told. Sheila was glad that he had thought to ask her name, but was surprised that it was a Hispanic name.

Since they were parked directly across the street, they decided to stay in the car until she came out. Steve did walk around the block to see where the back entrance was, in case she would exit that way.

Back in the car, they tried to plan how they should handle this. Steve wanted to call her family. He thought they should all come up to Taos to make the decision about how best to deal with this situation. Sheila was completely opposed to this idea. She proposed they follow Sarah home. Once she was in her own house, they would go to the door together and then the two sisters would come face to face. Steve said nothing; it was obvious he did not feel comfortable with this plan.

Around two p.m., Sheila let out a cry, "There she is! She is coming out!" Steve had been facing her as they talked. He quickly straightened up. They both kept watching Sarah as she waited in front of the restaurant. She spoke with some of the people as they came and went. On and off, she kept looking up the street in the direction their car was facing.

"Someone is going to pick her up." Steve was thinking out loud. "We have to get our car turned around."

He was too late. As he started up, Sarah was going toward the street and getting into a small tan car. Steve could not pull out as the cars were so close and left no opening. It did not help that he felt very nervous and that Sheila, in her distraught state, kept urging him to hurry.

"Hurry, please, please, hurry! We are going to lose her!"

He pulled out quite suddenly and almost had an accident. He could feel the animosity of the other driver as he surged ahead, and quickly turned his car around. He hoped a policeman wasn't watching him.

Sheila had been kneeling on the seat, watching the tan car go in the opposite direction. Now that he was going in the same direction, he heard her crying, "I don't see the car anymore! We lost her! Oh, God, why did we lose her?" She was crying now, great sobs from the depth of her soul. The sobs and emotion she had kept pent up in the restaurant and in the car had to be released. They were pouring forth and tearing at Steve's heart as much as her own.

He kept driving straight ahead, out of town. Both of them were looking on the side streets as they passed. Then Sheila saw that the tan car was still ahead of them. They both breathed a sigh of relief as they followed at a safe distance. Sheila calmed down now, wiped her eyes and her face and straightened herself up. Looking over at him, she whispered, "Thank you." He, too, wiped his eyes and they both smiled sheepishly at each other.

Soon, they were out of town and on the highway when Sheila said breathlessly, "Steve, where is she going? We are in the middle of nowhere. Does she live in Espanola or Santa Fe?" She was incredulous as she spoke these words. Steve was too tense to answer. It was hard to follow a stranger's car and not be conspicuous.

They were about thirty minutes out of Taos, coming into a small village. He did not even know the name of it until the tan car pulled into the post office parking lot. He read and spoke out loud at the same time: "Velarde, New Mexico."

As they went past, Sarah was going into the post office. "What shall we do?" Sheila kept saying. He stopped as soon as he could and waited on the side of the road, hoping they would still be going in the same direction. Sheila, again kneeling on the seat, looking back, announced, "She is coming out and getting in the car!"

He let them pass and get about a half mile away before he pulled on the road and followed. Before he could say anything, the car turned right onto a gravel road. "What do we do now?" he all but shouted.

"Keep following, only stay about the same distance you are," was the uncertain reply.

As Steve turned onto the gravel road, Angela turned to Sarah, who was looking at the mail, and with concern in her voice, said, "That car has been behind us ever since we left Taos. Now it is turning in here. Who could it be?"

Sarah had been preoccupied with a letter she had received from the convent. She looked back and shrugged her shoulders, replying, "They're probably just on a ride and want to get closer to the river. Don't worry, Angela, we will be home soon."

Angela dropped her off and watched as she walked up the long driveway to the house. The house faced the river and the mountains, so she waited for Sarah to walk around and wave from the porch before she started up. Looking in her mirror, she watched the car behind her pass Sarah's drive. She pulled off into her own driveway. Angela stood and looked intently as Sheila and Steve passed.

Going slowly by, Steve turned to Sheila and, smiling, said, "Well, now we know where she lives, and her name." He was much more confident as he turned around and headed back toward the house Sarah had entered.

They stopped a short distance from the house. They could see the porch. The small modest home looked so well-kept. The land was cleared. Some places they had passed had junk all around, but not here. Whoever lived here cared, and it showed. There were not any other houses close by. You could see some homes, but there were a few acres in between. Angela's house was about a mile down the road.

"It is beautiful here," Sheila said as she reached for Steve's hand. They took in all the mountains and land, the silence and peace that seemed to envelope the entire area. She let the peace permeate her whole being and felt strength coming back into her body. She breathed deeply several times and prayed for God to help them. Steve kept rubbing her hand and the two of them felt as though they were one.

They sat like this for about ten minutes when they saw Sarah come out on the porch. She looked in the direction of their car, turned and said something to someone inside and then bounced down the steps, her long hair tied back in a ponytail. She was putting a jacket on and heading toward the river. They watched until she was out of sight before Sheila spoke.

"Let's do it, Steve. This is perfect. She is gone for a little while. We will meet whoever is in the house and see what their reaction is to me."

Steve was in agreement; he did not know what else could be done. They drove in the driveway, parked and walked around and up the steps to the porch. Sheila had a jacket on now, but her disguise was gone. Her hair hung to her shoulders and her eyes told the story of the uncertainty she felt as Steve rapped.

Carmen opened the door, said, "Hello," and then gasped. "Oh, my God! Who are you?"

She had her hand held to her heart and a look of utter dismay and fear crossed her features.

"Ernest! Ernest!" she cried.

He was beside her in an instant and stared at the two strangers on the porch. As he regained his composure, he put his arm around Carmen. Opening the screen door, he said in a very husky voice, "Please come in."

Chapter 7

The house was so cozy and warm, but the four people standing and staring at each other felt chilled to the bone.

"I'm Sheila Farrell. Sarah is my twin sister, who was abducted when she was two days old from the hospital in Phoenix, Arizona. My parents have been heartbroken all these years. . . ."

This was too much for Carmen to take all at once; she almost collapsed. Ernest helped her into the dining room where they all sat down. He was so shaken himself and choked up, he could not speak.

Steve's eyes told Sheila to wait—she was going too fast. She understood and remained silent. They all sat there, with so much to say, but no one said a word. Instead, all of their concerns, emotions, and lives were flashing before them.

Sheila realized she had made a mistake in blurting out the story of her sister in four short sentences. She felt compassion for these people as she looked at them and realized that they were very good people. Carmen had taken a rosary out of her pocket and was holding it tightly. They both had honest eyes and their facial expressions showed only sincerity. There was a crucifix on the wall and on a stand underneath it stood a large statue of Our Lady of Fatima and a lighted candle.

Sheila got up and went to Carmen. Crying, she said, "I'm so sorry; I can see you are hurt and bewildered. So am I."

As soon as Carmen saw her tears and utter desolation, her motherly instinct took over and she hugged the girl who looked so familiar that she seemed to be her own daughter. They both cried. The two men were tearful also. They stayed near for when they were needed.

After several minutes, the women turned and went to their men. Both men put their arms around the one they loved dearly and comforted her. After a few seconds had gone by, Sheila started over.

"Please forgive me and help me to know how to handle this. Sarah will probably be coming back soon and I do not want to do to her what I've done to both of you."

Ernest motioned for them all to sit and asked Sheila to begin again, a little slower this time, and as briefly as possible. He, too, was thinking of Sarah.

Carmen cried and cried as she heard the story. Sheila had to stop many times as she, too, could not talk for the tears that would not stop flowing and the constricting lump in her throat.

Ernest cried on and off himself, as he, in turn, told them how they came to raise Sarah. The knock on the door that night so many years ago, when Laura first came with the baby. The story she told them. How they agonized over what to do, but wanted the baby so much, they decided to keep her. They knew nothing of a child being abducted in Phoenix, and did not know Sarah was a twin. They had believed Laura's story completely.

When he finished, Sheila said, "I believe everything you have told us. I see how much you love her and thank God she has been in your care, and that we have found her. What are we going to do now, though? Should we stay or should we go? If I do not meet with her now, it will still have to happen."

Carmen had been praying through all of this and said, "There is no better time than the present moment. God in His goodness will take care of everything." She got up and stood behind Ernest, putting her hands on his shoulders and looking at them, she said, "Sarah went to church to see Father Joseph. She will be home momentarily. Ernest, I think we should go out to meet her and explain to her what we have just learned. As hard as this is going to be, good will come out of it for all of us."

Sheila was looking so devastated, Carmen went to her. "You are right, it has to come out now or tomorrow or the next day. We would all be on edge the entire time." Turning to Ernest, she held out her hand, and the two of them walked out of the house, down the porch steps, and through the field toward the river. The two held hands tightly and talked of how they would tell Sarah.

"Ernest, help me. I feel an unbearable pain in my heart. What are we going to say to Sarah? How are we ever going to tell her she has an identical twin sister?" Then, almost in the same sentence: "Please, Blessed Mother, help us. Give us the words, help us all through this."

All Ernest said was, "There, there," as he patted her arm. "We will know what to say when we see her."

In the house, Sheila sat staring at her hands. Wondering what she would do, what she would say when they came face to face. Steve moved over to the couch and put his arm around her. She laid her head on his shoulder and wept quietly. "I probably should have called my parents. They should be here with us. This isn't working out at all and I don't know what else to do." He tried to comfort and encourage her the best he could.

"I liked what Carmen said: 'There is no better time than the present moment.' You'll know what to say when you see her."

"Steve, you do not understand, this is going to be harder for her than it is for me. I've known about her for almost a year. She is finding out about me now, tonight, at this very moment."

* * * * *

Sarah saw her parents coming to meet her. She knew something was wrong from the way they waved. She started to run, stopping just before she reached them.

They all looked at each other and Sarah, walking slowly now, asked in a deeply concerned voice, "What is it? What has happened?"

The three of them put their arms around each other. After they separated, her parents tried to tell her the story they had just heard.

"Sarah,. . . darling mija,. . . how do we tell you?"

"Mamacita, stop crying and tell me."

It was no use. Carmen couldn't go on. Ernest was so quiet, he barely could be heard. "Sarah, there is a young woman in our living room who says she is your sister. There is no doubt either, as, believe it or not, she is identical to you. Sarah, you have an identical twin sister."

Sarah gasped and tried to understand what she was being told. "How did she find me? Are you sure? What did she tell you?"

"A young man is with her. She is very shaken, as we are. She told us you were abducted when you were only two or three days old. It seems Laura lied to us. Everything she told us was a lie. She stole you from the hospital for money. . . ." Ernest couldn't go on.

Contrary to what Sheila thought, all of this was not as much of a shock to Sarah as it had been to her. Sarah knew she had other relatives out there someplace. The surprise was having a twin sister and having been kidnapped.

They were getting close to the house now. Steve saw them coming and told Sheila. When they walked in, she was standing, waiting for them to enter.

The two sisters stood and looked at each other. Neither of them moved. Their emotions were running very high as they took each other in. The exact features, hair, eyes, height, build. They held their breath.

Sarah had not shed a tear when she heard about her sister. Now she started to walk toward her and Sheila, too, moved slowly forward. They walked into each other's arms and, holding each other ever so gently, they cried many tears. They were tears of joy.

When they separated, Sarah walked over to her parents, took both of their hands and, with a reticent smile, tried to comfort them. "This is a traumatic experience for all of us. I love you both dearly. Still I am very happy to find out I have a twin sister. Try to look at it this way: Now, you have two daughters."

Chapter 8

After Sarah tried to console her parents, everyone seemed to feel a little more at ease.

Carmen, Ernest, and Steve all went to finish preparing the dinner that Carmen had started just before their unexpected visitors had arrived.

The two sisters retired into the parlor to talk. They couldn't believe they had found each other. Both shared how sometimes a strange loneliness would come upon them as though something was missing in their lives. Neither of them had been able to understand this strange feeling until now.

Sheila repeated the story to Sarah about how she had been abducted, and then brought her up to date on all the events that had happened in the last few months.

She was astounded to hear of the trust fund and of her inheritance. She couldn't believe that both of her real parents were alive and she had another sister, brother, sister-in-law, and two nieces. Her trust and confidence in God, along with her ascetic life of prayer made her less vulnerable than most as she heard briefly all of these facts. All through dinner, more and more was shared about the events leading up to finding her.

Ernest was fearful that Sheila and her family would not believe them. Maybe someone would think that they were the abductors. He worried about the fact that they were not able to prove that Laura gave them the baby. As he expressed his concern, fear came and went across Carmen's face. Sarah assured them there was nothing to worry about.

As they talked about all these things, Sheila expressed concern about Howard, Ellen, and the rest of the family. "We must call Dad and Mom and tell them." Complete silence followed this comment. All eyes turned and focused on Sarah.

Ernest and Carmen felt lumps come into their throats as she responded. "You have to realize that this has been a shock to my family, as well as for me. As far as I am concerned, they," and she gestured toward her parents. ". . . are, and always will be my real parents. Never could anyone or anybody, including my own flesh and blood, take their place. After all that has happened today, there is no way I could talk to them in the next day or two, let alone meet them."

She took a deep breath before going on. "I suggest that Steve go back to Santa Fe and you stay here with us in Velarde for a few days until we sort all this out."

Sheila started to object, but Sarah would hear none of it. Instead, she gently took her sister's hands into hers. "There is no other way as far as I am concerned. The first step that you and I must take is getting to know each other. We need time together. We look exactly alike, yet we are different. We have been raised in completely different cultures. We think differently, we believe differently. Neither of us know where the other is coming from. We need these few days together to sit down by the river and talk and become acquainted with each other. It is necessary for you to get to know my parents." She again gestured toward her parents. "During these few days, we will make plans to meet your parents. . . ." She halted before adding, "And mine."

After Sarah got all this out, no one said a word for quite a few minutes. The silence was at an unbearable stage when Steve broke everyone's reverie with, "Sarah's right." He paused. "This is Thursday. I will go home and come back on Sunday. We will all attend Mass together. By that time, maybe some decisions will already be made as to what the next step should be."

He knew the Montoyas were Catholic. The religious atmosphere in the house was definitely Catholic, with the crucifix, statues, votive light. He had noticed this as soon as he entered their warm and inviting home. Most of all, Carmen fingered the rosary from the first moment they all met.

So it was decided. Sheila walked out to the car with Steve. "My parents will be so upset that I have not called them right away." She was pleading for his advice, as she went on. "What should I do?

When you get back to Santa Fe, do you think you should call them and tell them everything that has happened? What about where I am? Should we go along with Sarah's idea about how to handle this?" As she talked, she had such a sober and solemn look; he wished he could somehow reassure her.

"I don't know the right thing to do. This is a very delicate situation. You cannot drag Sarah away from here and take her into your environment, expecting life will go on as though none of this has happened. I believe the best thing to do is respect her wishes. It will be hard on you, but I will be back on Sunday. You can call me if you need me before then. In the meantime, the two of you will be able to recapture some of the lost years you have missed." Then with new-found conviction, he went on. "Yes, I do believe this is right. It will be good for both of you and for the Montoyas."

Hugging her gently but firmly, he comforted her and whispered in her ear, "Your sister said, as we were leaving, 'Take one day at a time and all else will be provided'. You do that, too, and have confidence that in the end, everything will turn out right. She is a very deep young woman. It is good that she will not rush or be pushed into anything until she is ready."

Now, in the silence of the night, they just held each other. Separating slightly, he looked deeply into her eyes, communicating his love for her. Then, with deep emotion, he said very softly, "I love you very much. Will you marry me?"

Sheila, laying her head against his chest, started crying once again, but finally was able to get out, "Yes. I love you, too."

In bed that night, she could not get to sleep. She thought of Steve. She loved him so much. Her happiness was overwhelming as she thought of his proposal.

What a time to pick! she thought, with a slight smile lighting up her face. Then in the next instant, What better time could he have picked? She would never forget his gentleness or the love she saw in his eyes as he caressed her.

She turned on her side and stared at Sarah, already sound asleep next to her. It was so funny, as if she were staring at herself. It was like looking in a mirror. All of her features, everything was so identical, except for their skin color. She is so dark from the sun and I am so pale. Those were some of her last thoughts as she, too, slumbered off into a deep sleep.

Carmen and Ernest stayed awake half the night talking. Would everyone believe them? What would happen now with their Sarah? Her father being a prominent physician, her mother a socialite. Another sister. . . and a brother.

It was all so much to take in and to understand. How could they compete with all of this? They were so simple. Their life so simple and poor. . . yet so blessed.

They went to bed thanking God for all their blessings. Still they wondered. Would Sarah still enter the Carmelite Monastery?

Chapter 9

Early the next morning, Sarah went into the kitchen. Going directly to Carmen, she put her arms around her. "I love you, Mom. How about going to Mass with me this morning? It is beautiful out and we can talk on the way. I have something I want to tell you."

Carmen looked perplexed. "I'm in the middle of making tortillas. Dad will be in soon for breakfast, and what about Sheila?"

"Mom, we'll be back by eight o'clock. Dad will fix himself a plate when he comes in. Just leave a note and let's go."

Before they left, Sarah called Michael's, explaining that family circumstances would keep her from coming in for the last couple of days she was scheduled to work. She had already given her notice—Saturday the sixteenth would have been her last day. John thanked her and expressed how much all of them would miss her.

The day was so pleasant. They walked in silence to church. Sarah was the first to speak. "Mom, do you remember when I got home from work yesterday, before Sheila and Steve came into our lives, that I told you I received a letter from Mother Mary Gabriel?" Carmen was intrigued by what Sarah was about to say. "Well, a problem arose about my entering Carmel. Mother said I would need a copy of my birth certificate, and I remembered that you said you never had one for me. That is why I went to church last evening, to see Father Joseph. I prayed and I knew God would take care of it. My point is, Mom, I believe He has taken care of it. Divine Providence sent my real sister to me. Already the problem I thought I had yesterday is taken care of, as I'm certain my birth certificate is on file in Phoenix. What I want, though, more than anything else, is for you and Dad to see the good that can come out of this situation. God takes care of us. He knows our needs, even down to these simple daily problems that arise.

"Last night, the unexpected happened—an event that will change our lives. We can accept the changes that will happen because of it, or we can dwell on all the turmoil we feel. I'm not saying these next few days or few weeks will be easy. We will be meeting new people and encountering new situations. We will feel uneasy and sad. . . and joyful. Let God help us to see the way. Remember, if we take it one day at a time we can go through anything."

Putting her arm around Carmen's waist, she squeezed her. "Let's be happy, Mom. Let us take one day at a time. We can get to know Sheila a little, then her parents and family. The uneasiness will come and go, but if we let it, good will come from all of this."

Carmen looked at her daughter with such love. "You wanted to make me feel better and you have. I will tell Dad all of this, too. We will always be a family. Nothing and no one can change that." As they entered the church, they both smiled at each other and there was a peace in their hearts that showed outwardly.

Sheila woke up to an empty house. She arose and walked around, taking in everything. This house is so small, yet decorated in such good taste and has such a good tranquil feeling, she thought. Everything was clean and neat and the smell of homemade tortillas filled her nostrils as she entered the kitchen. She found the note on the table, read it, and then poured herself some coffee. The kitchen seemed to be the largest of all the rooms. The dining area took up one side of the room. It had a large round table. There was plenty of counter space, about four feet on one side and ten feet on the other. The sink faced out toward the side of the house with a large double window over it. The other window by the table faced the front looking out toward the river. Pale cream curtains with a light splash of daisies covered the windows, giving the room a feeling of warmth. They were pulled back, so that the sunlight filled the room, giving it a cozy atmosphere all its own.

What's next? she thought, as she sat at the table, nibbling on a tortilla.

The door opened and Ernest came in. He knew in a moment that his women had gone off to church. "All by yourself, huh?" he said as he poured some coffee and joined Sheila at the table. He started eating heartily. He had already been working for a couple of hours.

They both ate in silence. Sheila, seeing the concern written all over his face, tried to be helpful. "You'll like my parents and they'll like you. I hardly know you both, and already I feel very comfortable here. I believe everything you have told me, and so will my family. We are just so happy that we have finally found my sister after all these years."

Ernest was a man of few words, but he responded with cordiality, and resignation. "What will be will be. We will handle all of this to the best of our ability." He smiled at her. "It will all turn out." He had just finished speaking when Sarah and Carmen came in. They all had breakfast together and talked as though they had been part of each other's lives forever.

After breakfast, the two girls walked down to the river. The river was such an enormous part of Sarah's life. She would wade in it, or sit and look at it almost every day. The feeling she got from the river and its surroundings could not be put into words. She loved this area, this place. It was all a part of her and always would be. Today, they sat by the river in one of Sarah's favorite spots.

They talked about so many important things. Sheila could not contain herself any longer. "Steve asked me to marry him last night," she said, with great exhilaration.

Sarah beamed as she leaned over and hugged her tightly. "I, too, have some news that I want to tell you. I am so happy for you and Steve and I want you to feel this same happiness for me. What I am going to tell you, you will not understand at first. No one does. You must let me help you to understand—for it is my whole life. . . just as Steve will now be yours." As Sheila listened, she started to get a very uneasy feeling. They both sat in silence for a few minutes, then Sarah made her announcement. "I am going to be a nun."

For a few moments, Sheila said nothing. The silence became almost unbearable. What is she saying, what is she thinking about? The words almost burst out of Sheila, but she continued to sit silently, waiting for more information and looking at her sister with complete disbelief. She knew very little of what a nun was, but as far as she was concerned, Sarah could not be one.

Her attention came back fast as she heard her sister speak again. "I am supposed to enter the Carmelite monastery in Santa Fe on January nineteenth. It is a cloistered convent, which means I will live enclosed the rest of my life. I will not be able to come out once I have entered."

Sheila could not contain herself any longer. "NO!" she screamed.

"You can't be a nun. . . I just found you! Now you're saying in about four weeks I am going to lose you again! Are you crazy? Dad won't let it happen! He will stop you!" She didn't even realize that she was screaming. She stood up, crossed her arms over her chest and looked down at her sister.

Sarah arose, too, and put her arms around her in a futile gesture of comfort. When she spoke, however, her voice was full of resolve. "No one will stop me. It is the will of God. . . and mine, too."

Chapter 10

Sheila would not go back to the house. She insisted Sarah go and leave her to herself for a little while. Standing alone in the stillness of the day, she once again let out a piercing pain-filled cry and wailed, "Where are you, God? I do not seem to know You as she does, but I will not let You take her from me!" Sobbing and still talking out loud, she continued. "You did that once. . . why? Why did You let her be stolen from us for all these years? What about my parents?"

She dropped down to her knees, the same as Sarah did so often in prayer, but Sheila was in agony, not peace. She hammered the ground with her fists and kept yelling, "No, no, I don't understand! I don't want to understand! She can't do this! We will stop her! We will!" She cried until she was exhausted, then she tried to compose herself as much as was humanly possible before walking back to the house.

They were all waiting for her on the porch. Sarah had already told Carmen and Ernest what had happened. Sheila's face was swollen from tears.

Carmen went to her. "Mija, you are my little mija, too. Don't worry."

Sheila pulled away. "What kind of an influence have you had on my sister that she is going to put herself in a convent that she can never leave? Who ever heard of such a thing?" She said this with contempt and even a touch of bitterness. Sarah now was the one to go to her.

"Please, Sheila, calm down and be reasonable. You cannot condemn something you know nothing about. I know this is hard for you to understand now; someday you will. You told me that you and

Steve are getting married—how would you feel if I was acting this way over your love for him, and his for you? How would you feel if I was completely against your marrying Steve and spending the rest of your life with him?"

Sheila spun around, ashen, and with a voice steeled to protect herself, said, "There is simply no comparison! I will never understand this! I am leaving here right now and I'm calling Dad and Mom. I should have done that right away." She hurried into the bedroom that she, just last night, had shared with Sarah for the first time.

Slamming the door, she flung herself on the bed and sobbed. She couldn't help it; all the pent-up emotions of the last few months were released in the heavy sobs that filled her throat, and came out in unrelenting agony.

Sarah and her parents stood silently and looked hopelessly at each other. The sobs penetrated the house, and tears ran freely down Sarah's face as well. Instinctively, the three moved together and embraced each other. They did not even realize for how long. It was the incessant ringing of the phone that had Ernest move away from them. Whoever it was had hung up by the time he reached it.

Now the house was quiet. The sobs had ceased coming from behind the bedroom door. Sarah entered her room. Sheila was lying on her back, staring at the ceiling, her hands folded across her chest. Sarah went to the bed. Sitting on the edge, she bent over so that she was looking directly into Sheila's eyes. She placed her hand on her sister's, and, filled with great emotion, she whispered, "I love you. I can feel your hurt, your pain. We have two hearts and bodies but we are actually one when it comes to emotions and love."

Sheila just looked back at her, lying so still you might think she was dead if you were not looking into her eyes—eyes that were searching into Sarah's. . . into her very being. Sheila was still now and felt a deep calm she couldn't understand. She believed deeply that Sarah's heartfelt prayers were the cause of it.

She lifted herself up and put her arms around Sarah and the two of them clung to each other. Strength surged through Sheila, coming from the loving embrace that Sarah was giving her. She finally spoke in a husky voice. "I'm sorry, I don't understand. I apologize for having acted as I did."

They were holding each other in an embrace that seemed to be healing her in some way. Sarah encouraged her. "We do not have to let this unpleasant episode separate us. We can still spend a few days with each other and then go see your Mom and Dad—our parents."

Pulling away now, Sheila said, "That's the first time you've actually admitted that they are your parents, too."

There was a long silence. "I always knew my paternal father was most likely living someplace else and I thought my mother was dead. For me, Carmen and Ernest will always be my true mother and father, they could never take second place. Now that I know my real parents are both alive and that I have another family, I am actually looking forward to meeting them.

"What I want you to do, Sheila, is learn to accept each day with its ups and downs. Now that we have found each other, nothing will ever take us apart. We will live our own lives, make our own world, but we will never have lost years again, as you expressed earlier. Sheila, what I want you to comprehend deeply is that neither one of us actually have had lost years. You were raised by parents who loved you dearly and so was I. We might have been miles apart, as far as physical distance is concerned. But we were never miles apart within our hearts. We both felt each other's soul without knowing what or who it was we felt. Divine Providence has now brought us together to help me enter the monastery and to help you settle down with Steve. We don't have to wonder anymore. When we have faith and trust God, His Divine wisdom takes care of all these trials of life for us. We just have to place ourselves in His hands and, unafraid, move into each new day, whatever it holds for us.

"Do you understand anything that I am saying, dear Sheila? Dearest sister, will you try to understand and accept what you cannot change? Will you accept me and love me for what I am and for what I want to become? You do not have to understand now. You will in time."

Sheila could not believe how differently she felt as she listened to Sarah. A peace entered her soul and heart. She knew that it was her sister talking, but she felt a tremendous power behind the words, a magnetism that made her accept, without question, what was being conveyed to her.

Chapter 11

Steve hung the phone up. He had let it ring and ring, hoping someone would finally answer. He had decided on the way home from Velarde that he would take it upon himself to fly to Phoenix and explain to the Farrells what had happened in the last few days. He felt confident that he was right and he knew Sheila would agree with him. His flight left in a few minutes. He would arrive in Phoenix in a couple of hours. Richard Farrell was picking him up at the airport. Richard was already wondering what the urgency was, and where Sheila was.

Steve had been so evasive with him, because the last thing he wanted was for Richard to start popping questions at him that he did not want to answer. Until he talked with Sheila, he shouldn't have done anything. He was remonstrating himself, wondering why he had called Richard so soon. He had meant well. He thought he would tell Richard everything, and then the both of them could go to the Farrells with the news. He had not counted on the way things were turning out.

He had not been able to talk to Sheila first, and now he was in a very awkward position. He wondered what to say when he met Richard in Phoenix.

Darn, darn, he kept repeating to himself. What made me make these reservations and call Richard before I talked to Sheila? He wanted to call her once more, but he heard the last call for flight 713, leaving for Phoenix. As it was, he had to run to get to the gate at the very last minute.

All the way to Phoenix, Steve was uneasy about the task he was taking upon himself. He had reasoned it out and felt confident in his decision. He still felt this would be so much easier for all concerned. How could the two girls just walk in on the Farrells? How could Sheila just call and tell them on the phone? Why didn't someone answer when he called?

When he got off the plane, sure enough, there was Richard, full of questions. "Where is Sheila? What is going on, Steve?"

Steve stopped and faced him squarely. "Richard, give me a few minutes. I need to talk to Sheila and then I will be able to answer your questions." He was looking at his watch as he was speaking. It was five-fifty p.m. "Get a beer in the lounge. I'll be there in a few minutes."

As they sat down to dinner, Carmen was relieved that Sheila had regained her composure. They had been eating and talking for several minutes when the phone interrupted them. Ernest answered it.

"Ernest, this is Steve. I would like to speak to Sheila. . . . Hello, darling," he started and, in a very few words, brought her up-to-date on what was going on.

Sheila felt relief surging through her. She agreed with him completely concerning his decision. Steve continued. "I am going to tell Richard right now and then we will go see your parents either tonight or first thing in the morning. Preferably in the morning, unless Richard has already announced my coming. Then they will call you and make plans for the next step."

"Thank you, Steve. I love you so much and I need you. I need to talk to you, to tell you about all that has happened here. You won't believe it." Her voice sounded anxious. "I can't do it on the phone. Please be with my parents when we all meet."

"You know I will be there for you, Sheila. Whatever the decision is or wherever they decide to meet, I will be there, darling, for you. I love you dearly."

Sheila went back to the dinner table and told them everything that Steve had told her. The four of them looked at each other with relief. It was Sarah who said, "Let us pray for Steve and for all of them." They took hands and bowed their heads. It was now Friday evening at approximately six twenty p.m.

Sarah thought, "So very much has happened in the last twenty-four hours." She quietly lifted her head and looked at Sheila who still had her head bowed in prayer.

She is so sophisticated, so different than I am. Her eyes moved toward Ernest and Carmen and she felt a quiet peace and happiness.

They were so devout, so real, so unsophisticated, and yet refined, so poor, yet not poor. What would they think when they found out that she was an heiress? She couldn't believe it herself. Money was very hard to come by on the farm, but their joy did not depend on money, so they were always happy.

She smiled outwardly as she realized that money would not matter to them at all. Only her happiness would be of the utmost importance to them. How would her real parents take to her entering the convent? Would it be as hard for them as for Sheila?

Closing her eyes, she said a silent prayer that they would all learn to love and understand each other. When she opened her eyes the three of them were staring at her. She could do nothing but smile. She had confidence that her prayer would be granted.

Chapter 12

Richard called Sue and told her he would be late coming home. The two men talked for a couple of hours. Steve went home with him for the night. Over a late dinner, they filled Sue in. They had decided to wait until morning before telling Howard, Ellen, and Leah.

After showing Steve to his room, Richard called his parents. It was after ten p.m.

"Dad, I know it's late, but knowing you sometimes play golf early on Saturday I wanted to call. Sue and I will be over for breakfast with you and Mom around eight. Steve is in town and he will be joining us. . . Dad, wait—we will answer any questions in the morning, okay? See you then."

Setting the phone back in its cradle, Richard rubbed the back of his neck and let out a deep breath. Sue came to him and putting her arms around his waist, suggested he call Leah.

Leah answered in a very sleepy voice. "Richard, what is the matter?"

"Leah, I need you to meet us at Dad and Mom's at eight a.m. and don't tell them anything. This is about Sarah. Wait, Leah, wait. . . listen. I know this isn't fair to you. I don't know what else to do, otherwise we will be up all night. Try and go back to sleep and wait until morning."

He paused, listening to his sister protest strongly and understood her feelings. He interrupted. "Okay, come over, bring some clothes and plan to stay here tonight. Sue and I will be waiting for you and then we will tell you what has happened." As tired as Richard was, he knew it was only fair to Leah. He would be reacting in the same way as she was under the circumstances.

Howard hung up the phone and turned to Ellen, who was waiting to hear who it was.

"Richard," he said casually, "wanting to tell me they would be here for breakfast with us in the morning." He kept his voice matter-of-fact and light. Inside, though, he knew something was going on. He didn't want Ellen up all night worrying. So, out of concern for his wife, he showed no sign of what he was thinking or feeling.

Leah arrived at Richard's in a state of breathless expectancy. She tried to remain as poised as possible, but she had all she could do to control her feelings.

On the surface, Richard and Sue seemed calm, but Leah perceived instantly how tense her brother was. This did not help her state of mind, which by now was running away with itself. She had already conjured up all sorts of thoughts, and had to keep telling herself, "Wait and see what Richard has to say before you assume that all these things you are thinking and feeling are true."

It seemed like an eternity to Leah before they were finally in the parlor with a cup of coffee. She was sitting in anticipation, waiting eagerly to hear the incident that led up to Richard's call.

When she first arrived, they went through all the motions of getting her settled in her room and a dozen other immaterial things before they were finally face to face.

It was extremely evident that Richard was having a hard time knowing where to begin. Leah finally said, "Richard, will you just blurt it out? Whatever it is, I can't wait a moment longer to know!"

"It is not easy, Leah, and how in heaven's name am I going to tell Dad and Mom when I don't even know how to tell you?" He once again rubbed the back of his neck. "Why couldn't you wait until morning so I could say all of this once?"

Leah held her breath, waiting quietly now until Richard said in a deep, husky voice, "Sheila and Steve found Sarah! She is living near Taos, New Mexico. It seems she has always lived there."

Leah was exuberant. "Thank God, after all this time. . . ."

"Yes, Leah, it is wonderful, but according to Steve, she doesn't want her real parents. She is happy and content where she is and she believes the people who raised her will always be her only true parents. Now, how do I tell Dad and Mom that? She doesn't even want to see them right away. She wants to get to know Sheila first. Do you think we are going to be able to keep Dad and Mom from going to her immediately? I don't think so."

Leah and Sue both looked overwhelmed at Richard's outburst. Leah looked like she was going to cry. Sue went over to her. Putting her arms around her sister-in-law, she responded, "Richard, it all looks worse tonight. It is so late and we have all heard news we never expected to hear. It will look better in the morning. Remember, Steve did say he would be back with Sheila and Sarah on Sunday. This is hard for everyone. No one knows what to say or do, let alone how to decipher their own feelings."

Sue's words seemed to bring comfort to both Leah and Richard. He slowly got up and, going to them, he put his arms around them both. With renewed courage, he said, "You're right. It will all work out. It will take time, but somehow it will all work out. The important thing is, Sarah was lost and now, thank God, she is found."

Chapter 13

Howard was awake all night long. He sensed something was up. Richard sounded vague and uncertain on the phone. Howard knew they were coming to breakfast for a reason. Being unable to sleep, he was up and out for a brisk walk around the grounds early in the morning.

When he got back, Ellen was already in the dining room, fussing over the table and engaged in giving Martha some last minute details about the meal.

She was delighted when she saw him. "I'm really going to enjoy having them eat with us this morning, and you, too," she said, with a twinkle in her eye as she reached up and planted a kiss on his cheek. "What's wrong, Howard? You seem a little stiff this morning. I was only joking about you being here, instead of on the golf course."

He took her in his arms and gave her a loving, gentle kiss. "Let's talk some before they arrive, Ellen." Looking at his watch, he went on, "We only have a few minutes."

A little concerned, she poured coffee and sat across the table from him with anticipation. "Ellen, I have this feeling that something is amiss or about to happen. We need to prepare ourselves that the children are not just popping in to see us and have breakfast with us. There is a purpose for them coming this morning. I did not want to worry you or keep you awake during the night so I said nothing, but now I want you to know, to be prepared for whatever it is." With this he shrugged his shoulders and reached for her hands. Cupping them in his, he continued, "Don't worry, dear, maybe I'm wrong, but I want you to be prepared, in case I'm right about this interior feeling I have."

Ellen looked lovingly at her husband. He always put her first; her interests, her feelings. He was always there to help her, to give her guidance and understanding. Now as they stared into each other's eyes, they felt, without uttering a word, the vast love they had for each other. "Howard, I love you. Whatever it is, with your help, I'll be able to handle it." Her voice trailed off into barely a whisper as their children came into the room. Steve was with them.

Ellen searched her children's faces and knew immediately that Howard was right. After the initial greetings, they all sat down to eat. Ellen met Howard's eyes several times during the meal. She needed his strength to be able to converse freely and wait patiently for whatever was to come.

When they were almost finished, a lull came into the conversation. It was almost unbearable. The silence engulfed them before Richard was able to bring himself to speak. "Mother, we have some news for you and Dad. It is good news, but it may also bring you some apprehension or distress."

Leah was fidgeting by this time. She got up and moved close to her mother. "Richard, let me tell them." She paused. "Sheila and Steve found Sarah."

Howard and Ellen looked into each other's eyes. They did not say anything. It was as if they could not comprehend what was being said. Neither one of them expected this piece of news. They didn't know if they felt relieved, or happy, or sad. They could not feel anything, the shock was so great. After the initial shock wore off, their questions began. Where? Where was she found? Where is Sheila now? Endless questions which only Steve could answer, but in a very limited manner. He had so little information. He told them briefly how he and Sheila came to find Sarah.

"I told Sheila I had seen someone that looked so much like her, but I couldn't remember where. Then a couple of days ago, through a chance meeting with a friend, my subconscious was triggered and it came back to me. We did not want to give you another false hope, so we decided to wait to see if it was really her. We found her working in a restaurant in Taos. We followed her home. When she came out and left the house for awhile, we went to the door and rang the bell. It was a shock to her parents, the Montoyas, as soon as they saw Sheila. We talked and after Sarah returned, the two girls finally met. It was a very touching moment."

He explained everything that had happened. How good Sarah looked, all about their meeting with Ernest and Carmen. He told all he knew, which seemed so little.

By now Howard and Ellen were so excited. What should they do? They wanted to see their daughter. To go to her now.

The excitement kept growing for all of them. Steve explained how Sarah had said she needed to get to know Sheila first. Howard decided, after one look at Ellen, that they would have none of it. They were going to go to Taos, or Velarde, or wherever their daughters were. Steve interrupted.

"I told Sheila I would be back there tomorrow morning, hopefully in time to go to Mass with Sarah and her family."

Ellen stiffened at hearing about Sarah's family. She knew she was not being reasonable; after all, to Sarah, these people were her family. Regardless, she was crying inside. We are her family! We must go to her, to both of them, and be with them! She turned and abruptly said just that. "We are her parents and we will go to her."

Howard was by her side in an instant. "It's all right, sweetheart, everything is all right. Have courage. We will go. We will meet our daughter after twenty-two years. We will finally see the one that we have yearned to hold all this time. The main thing is that she is alive. She has been happy and cared for." His voice trailed off as he held Ellen in his arms, the feeling in both of their hearts was one of overwhelming helplessness.

It was mid-afternoon by the time Richard had made all the travel arrangements for the family. Leah and Steve were going with Howard and Ellen to New Mexico. Richard and Sue would wait to hear from them before making a decision as to what they would do. He was able to get seats for them on a flight arriving in Albuquerque at nine p.m. that night. He arranged to have a car waiting for them.

The last thing he did was have Steve call Sheila. This time, Richard talked with her. "Sheila, Dad and Mom will not wait to come. Maybe it is a little premature, but who can blame them after all these years? What I would like you to do is to tell Sarah that I'd like to speak with her. I will tell her about Mom and Dad."

There was a long pause; then Richard heard a woman's voice that sounded confident and secure. The voice sounded a whole lot like Sheila's, saying "Hello, Richard."

"Sarah, as you know, I am your brother. This is a very delicate situation for you, I am sure. However, Dad and Mom cannot wait to come and see you. They want to come now. Surely, you can understand that?"

A longer pause ensued, then, "Are you sure they should come here right now? It was only two days ago Sheila and I met for the first time."

"I don't think anyone knows how to handle this, Sarah. I'm sure we all have mixed emotions. Why not get started on meeting each other and talking things out? Nothing is going to happen overnight, but we all must begin sometime. It seems there is no time as good as the present."

Sarah was silent for a long time. Richard didn't push her; he waited quietly for her to respond to what he had said. Finally, she asked, "Where will they stay? Our house has only two bedrooms. Otherwise, they would be welcome to stay right here. I know Dad and Mom would want them to, if it were possible."

Richard interrupted. "Don't worry about that. I will make reservations for them in Taos. . . ."

Now it was Sarah who cut in. "No, Richard, Espanola is much closer to us, or better still, they can stay in Santa Fe, at Sheila's. Instead of arriving tonight, I think it would be much wiser for them to plan on arriving here in Velarde around one p.m. tomorrow. We will all meet then, and this way, my mother can have a nice dinner ready for all of us."

Richard winced when she said "my mother", thinking of their own mother. Despite this, he understood Sarah's loyalty to her mother. He felt good talking to Sarah and he knew that the only way for all of them to feel peaceful was to meet and talk. "That's good thinking, Sarah. They are going to be quite tired by the time they arrive in Albuquerque. It will be too much for them to drive up to Taos, Santa Fe is best. . . yes, Steve is right here. I will put him on. First, though," and now Richard's eyes filled up with tears, "I want you to know we all love you. None of us ever believed—deep in our hearts—that we would ever find you. Be patient with us, if we can't fully understand you at this time. We will be patient with you, if you do not understand us."

Sarah, who had been so steadfast in all of this, now felt the tears roll down her cheeks. She knew they would not be able to understand her decision to enter the convent at this time, nor for a long time. She thought back about Sheila's reaction to her becoming a nun and felt there would be much misunderstanding before they would all be able to reach the clarity and emotional stability that Richard was talking about.

"Richard, I do not know what to say, but I will be looking forward to seeing them." Richard handed the phone back to Steve. "Steve, thank you for being the go-between for Sheila and me. Everything has to take its course now—for all of our lives. I want to congratulate you. Sheila has told me that you asked her to marry you. I am very happy for you both and now I will put Sheila back on the phone. I must go and prepare my parents for tomorrow."

Sheila had been standing right by her sister for the entire phone conversation. As Sarah turned toward her, she still had tears glistening in her eyes. They looked steadily at each other and knew that the bond they felt so strongly at this moment had been with them since birth.

Chapter 14

Velarde was cold and snowy Sunday morning. Snow had covered the ground and was still falling steadily. Sarah was so excited; she loved the snow. Looking from the bedroom window, she could see snow right up to the river's edge. The river looked cold and beautiful as the snow flakes hit it and were immediately swallowed up.

Sheila snuggled under the covers. She felt so warm and cozy and happy this morning. She watched her sister as she went around the room preparing for Mass. It was too early to be awake, she thought, yet she was wide awake as she lay there listening to Sarah tell her stories about the farm, and about the joys of growing up here in this small community.

They both shared skiing stories and marveled at how many times they skied in Taos. How could they have missed each other?

"What about Santa Fe? Do you go there often?" Sheila asked as she propped up her pillows and drew herself up into a warm comfortable position.

"We go to Santa Fe probably two to four times a year. It is always a big event for us when we go. Mom has a sister living there. We stay with her. We always have such a good time and we would like to go more often, but we can't afford to. We stock up on groceries and supplies, go to the dentist if necessary. We try to get everything in we need to do and then some fun things, too." Sarah was once again looking out the window at the river, and now she had a faraway look. Even as she finished speaking, you could see she was deeply engrossed in memories. Turning so she could see Sheila, she went on.

"Once, when I was eleven years old, I had to spend three weeks in the hospital in Santa Fe and over a month at my aunt's house before I was able to come home. My friend, Angela, and I were sleigh riding right over there." She turned and looked out once again as she pointed to a distant hill. Sheila pulled herself forward until she could see it, then snuggled quickly back in to her pillow, pulling the blankets up around her as she listened.

"It was snowing, just like this, and it was so cold. It was a Sunday," she reminisced. "I even remember the day—January fifth. Angela and I and a few others had been sleigh riding for about an hour. There was ice on the river but it wasn't frozen solid. I remember how fast the sled was going and how close the river was. . . then before I knew what happened, I was on the ice.

"A boulder was in front of me and I knew I was going to hit it. Just before I did, I felt something or someone—I believe it was my guardian angel—turn the sled so I did not hit the boulder head on. The pain in my side and stomach was sickening as I felt the ice break under me. In an instant, I was under the water. When I came up for air, I still had a hold of the sled's rope, which was caught on the boulder.

"The rushing water tried to pull my body with it as I clung to the rope. Angela somehow threw the belt from her jacket to me and, with the help of the others, pulled me out. We still do not know how they managed to get me out, but, oh, how I prayed for help! They put me on the sleigh and pulled me home. I was freezing and in pain. My mother checked me over, and got me into warm pajamas. I said I was all right. There were no marks on me at all, so none of us knew that I was bleeding internally. She let me go to my room and rest, since that is what I wanted to do.

"Then a miracle happened. I was so sick I could not breathe. I could not see. I just lay there. Dad and Mom were having an egg burrito and she asked Dad to see if I wanted one. Before he reached my door, she was running past him with a thermometer in her hand. Somehow, as he was walking towards my bedroom, she felt an urgency that something was really wrong, so she did the only thing she knew. She took my temperature. It was ninety-four degrees. They both knew then that they must get me to the hospital immediately. Dad warmed up the old truck and Mom," Sarah laughed, "she decided I had to be clean so she washed me up.

"I was out of it. They rushed me to the hospital. Even though it was farther, they took me to St. Vincent's Hospital in Santa Fe. Our doctor lived there, and Mom's sister did, too, so she had a place to stay while I was in the hospital. Dad had to come home to work, but he came over one or two days a week. A priest friend of ours got to the hospital shortly after we arrived and Dad heard the doctor tell Father Ryan to do whatever he had to do because he believed I would not survive the operation. Father gave me the last rites of the Church.

"The three of them—Dad, Mom, and Father Ryan—waited in the small waiting room outside the operating room. Mom had her rosary in hand. They were all praying. She looked at the two of them. They were grieving. She told them not to worry, that I was going to be all right. They said nothing because neither of them could bring themselves to tell her what the doctor had said. It was half way through the operation when the doctor had one of the surgical nurses come out of the operating room and tell them I was going to make it. They were all very thankful to God and the Blessed Mother. Father Ryan made them go home to my aunt's house to get some rest, but he stayed with me all night, praying. I had tubes and needles all over me and was in intensive care for several days. I had ruptured my liver and had to have all but a small piece removed. They took out my gall bladder and my appendix. Even when I could come home to Velarde, I had to recuperate for over two months.

"Mom brought my school work home during those months. They put a bed right out near the large window in the living room so I wouldn't be cooped up in my room during the day and so I could see my beloved river and mountains." She finished, saying, "The view is good from this window, but better from the one out there."

Then hesitating a little, she continued, "All the nuns at the Carmelite monastery prayed for me to live. My mother called them the day I had the accident. As I told you before, all through the years, whenever we went to Santa Fe, we always went to Mass at Carmel and visited with the nuns. Whenever anyone needed prayers, we would call the sisters. Their prayers were answered many times.

"It was during my convalescence that the thought kept coming to me to enter Carmel, Our Lady of Mt. Carmel's order. At first, I didn't pay too much attention to it, but it kept coming back. I found myself wanting to pray more. I asked for "The Lives of the Saints" and a prayer book and other good books. My Aunt Rose has a large book collection in her home so when I went there for a month I was able to read books that inspired my heart with faith. I read about the last four things; death, judgement, heaven, and hell.

"Then I asked myself, what did I really want to do with my life? God had spared it; maybe He did want me to become a nun. I never lost that desire. From then on, I knew that someday, I would enter the monastery."

Sheila said nothing, but now instead of avidly listening as she had been, she moved as though she were uncomfortable with what her sister had said.

Sarah understood. In silence, she went back to looking out the window at the river.

Chapter 15

Ernest and Carmen were having a hard time dealing with everything that was happening. They knew there was nothing they could do but accept it and be there for Sarah whenever she needed them. Sarah always told them "One day at a time" or "Trust God, He will take care of everything". They were finding this advice very hard at the moment. Anticipating the meeting of Sarah and her real parents, they knew that this was the last thing they wanted to do today.

Carmen kept repeating herself to Ernest. "I don't know how I am going to handle this. I'm worried and have this inner turmoil that will not go away."

As usual, Ernest was right there for her, taking her in his arms and reassuring her over and over again. He was so patient and understanding and gentle with Carmen. He could fully understand her feelings, as he, too, felt very uncomfortable.

He sat at the table, drinking coffee, as they continued talking. Carmen prepared dinner. She felt so concerned about the meal. These people were well-to-do. . . how would they accept her simple meal? Then the thought crossed her mind, No one is going to want to eat, anyway, so why am I bothering? Why am I so uptight about it? Please, Lord, help me to be calm and accept all of this as part of Your Divine Plan as Sarah tells us we should do. Lord, that all sounds good, but I find it very hard at this time.

Turning to Ernest, she spilled out her feelings once again. "I don't even have any matching dishes or silverware, for that matter! I can't even begin to set a table like they are used to!"

Ernest started laughing. Carmen turned toward him in disbelief, then after looking at him in utter consternation, she, too, burst out into peals of laughter. It broke the tension. She walked over to Ernest and put her hands on his shoulders.

"Thank you for that," she said. "None of this is important. We have served many meals that everyone has enjoyed on our dishware. The important thing is family. Pray that somehow, we can all be family."

Ernest patted her hand. "Time will tell. Time will tell," was all he would say. In his heart, though, he was praying as earnestly as he knew how. Carmen, knowing him so well, understood his curt reply. She quietly went back to cooking, but the apprehension was quieted and her heart felt much calmer.

* * * * *

Ellen and Howard were in much the same dilemma. Arriving in Santa Fe a little before midnight, neither of them was able to get much more than a couple of hours of sleep and their nerves were running high. Leah tried hard to keep herself somewhat composed and be there for them. Question after question formed in their minds. Who were these Montoyas? How did they really get their daughter? Were they telling the truth? Could it be possible they were the actual abductors? They turned these questions over, first in their minds and then, out loud.

When they met Steve in the dining room at the hotel for breakfast, they explained their fears to him. Steve kept reassuring them that he fully believed Ernest and Carmen. They were good, sincere people; it was very evident. They would see for themselves when they met. Sarah was happy and seemed well-adjusted.

Howard exclaimed, "It is most likely as hard for them as it is for us! They must be having their own doubts and fears about us. After all, this is not the most comfortable situation for any of us. We must try and control ourselves and take things as they come." He reached for Ellen's hands and looked at her with much attention and concern. He felt her anxiety and knew how high-strung she was. How could he help her? he wondered. What could he do to ease the anxiety he saw in her?

Then the thought came to him: Just be here for her, hold her hand, comfort her with your understanding and love. Do what you are doing now.

Ellen saw the love in her husband's eyes and her tension started to ease. We will do this together, she thought, as we always have all of our lives.

Ellen and Howard had faith, yet neither of them thought consciously to pray. They didn't think to ask God to take them through this milestone in their lives.

However, God, Who alone knows all hearts, heard their silent prayer of turmoil and frustration. They did not even know that they were praying and that they were being heard by God. God, Who knows all, hears all, and loves all had already sent out His angels to help the Farrell and Montoya families.

* * * * *

Setting the table for dinner, Sheila and Sarah were both lost in their own thoughts. What surprise they would have felt if they had known how close their thinking was.

Lost in concern for their parents, neither of them thought much about their own feelings. Sheila could not wait to see Howard and Ellen. Sarah, on the other hand, could only think about Ernest and Carmen. Their hearts were filled with love for their own parents. If only they could have seen ahead and seen God's divine providence for them! If they could have seen His great love and understand His way. Then, and only then, would they have experienced that peace which is beyond all understanding.

Now, in this present moment, no one knew exactly what to do, how to feel, what to say. There was nothing better to do than let God, in His time, take care of everything. Given time, all things eventually work out.

As Ernest said, "Time will tell. Time will tell."

Chapter 16

The trip to Velarde was slow as the snow fell heavily. The snowfall was making the visibility difficult for Steve as he drove along the icy roads.

All of them were caught up in their own thoughts as they drove along. Ellen was thinking how she would greet her daughter, Sarah. What should her first words be? Should she run into her arms or be reserved? Would Sarah want her to embrace her? Would she be warm toward them? Would it be best to keep the conversation casual or personal? What would she say to these people her daughter had lived with all these years? What would their reaction be toward them? On and on her thoughts ran until they were at such a momentum that she turned in confusion and looked at her husband. He seemed so calm and serene. What were his deep feelings about all this?

Her anticipation was intense as Steve told them that they were getting close to Velarde. Howard's lips quivered; when Ellen saw this, she knew then that he was experiencing some of the same emotions that she was. She reached out for him and held his hand. Nothing was expressed verbally; the silence of the moment was vibrant with a passion that was hard to control.

The car turned down a small narrow road. Houses were spaced at quite a distance. They were small farms. The vastness of the surrounding area had a calming effect on the four of them as they pulled into the driveway of a very modest home. To Ellen, it seemed like this place was out in the wilderness.

The snow had subsided but the lingering beauty of it on the mountains and on the barren land was awesome. They sat in the car for a few moments and took it all in. Ernest opened the door and walked out onto the porch, patiently waiting for them to disembark from the car so he could greet them.

Steve was the first to open his door and come around to help Leah out. Howard followed and took Ellen's arm. They took a deep breath, and let it all out. Then the four of them made their way through the snow and up the steps to come face to face with Ernest.

As Steve introduced Howard, Ellen and Leah, Howard's hand went out to Ernest in a friendly and very firm grasp. Ellen just nodded her head toward him, and Leah seemed at a loss as to what to do.

"Come in, come in, we will freeze if we stand out here much longer. Carmen, they are here," Ernest called as they entered the small living room and stood looking at the three women inside.

Ellen put her hand to her heart as she stared at her daughters. A lump was in her throat that kept her from speaking. It seemed like an eternity that they all stood and stared at each other. It was actually only a moment before Carmen came forward.

"Please, take your coats off and warm yourselves." Her eyes were warm and her voice and manner welcomed them, helping to put them more at ease.

Sarah moved forward gracefully, taking both Ellen's and Howard's hands. Their eyes met in a steady gaze for a few seconds. Then Sarah embraced them both.

Pulling away, she smiled warmly and with her witty sense of humor and a twinkle in her eyes said, "I'm your daughter, Sarah." Everyone laughed slightly, helping to break the tension. Howard hugged Sarah, then Ellen held her close and found it hard to let her go. Howard helped by gently turning Sarah toward Leah and the two sisters silently embraced. Leah was visibly shaking and Ellen put her arm around her as the girls parted.

Steve had gone directly to Sheila and embraced her. The two of them watched the scene before them unfold. Ernest, too, had his arm around Carmen and they seemed lost in the real life drama that they found themselves immersed in.

Sheila went to her mom and dad and embraced them, then reached for Leah's hand and squeezed gently. Everyone was very uneasy. Sheila could find no words for all the emotion that she felt.

Sarah was bringing everyone together as though nothing extraordinary was happening. Before any of them realized it, coats were being shed and the Farrells were being ushered to the couch. Sheila and Sarah sat in chairs directly across from them.

Ernest served everyone hot apple cider and tried to exchange some pleasantries that soon became very stiff as the women sat in silence. Ellen was sitting on the edge of her chair. Her heart was pounding so hard she could barely breathe. She could not take her eyes off of Sarah. She could not speak. Her thoughts were centered on herself, Howard, and their children. . . until Carmen went by with a cup of cider for Steve. As she glanced at up Carmen, she saw a solitary tear running down her cheek and Ellen was finally able to breathe as the impact hit her: This woman is suffering as much as I am.

Before she was aware of what she was doing, she was on her feet. As Carmen turned, Ellen stood before her. Their eyes met and Ellen reached out to Carmen, touching her arm. Instantly, they embraced and tears poured down both of their cheeks. They tried to talk to each other but no words would come. Sarah rose and went to them.

When they felt her touch, they spontaneously turned to her and the three of them embraced. Sheila was so choked up, she did not know what to do. She knew how hard this was for her mother. Carmen, Sarah, and she had already been through this very scene. Before she could even think of being left out, Sarah reached for her and drew her up into the circle.

Although the men were sensitive to what was going on, as was Leah; they remained in the background. They felt it best to let the four women feel free to be together in the tenderness of the moment. So many emotions were being felt by all in that little living room on this cold December day, but each person there felt better now, as loving warmth was filling each of their own hearts.

Soon they were all avidly listening to one another as the story of Sarah's abduction was being retold by each side.

The Farrells sat on the edge of their chairs as Carmen and Ernest related the story of how they came to have Sarah.

Carmen began, "Laura's mother was a third cousin to Ernest, so we were not close and through the years saw very little of them. Now I realize that Laura's whole story was a lie, but then we believed her. She told us she had a boyfriend and he didn't want the baby. She didn't want her mother and father to know about the baby."

Ernest broke in. "That was to keep us from contacting anyone in Phoenix and possibly hearing anything about a baby girl named Sarah being abducted."

"You're right!" Carmen interrupted excitedly. "We have no TV and we listen to old records rather than the radio. She knew if she could keep us away from Phoenix, we would never question her story about the baby being hers. That's why she reminded us so many times about her parents. Her mother, having no time for an infant because of her work, and her father being an alcoholic who abused his family." Carmen's heart was pounding as she saw the Farrells gravely listening to her. Neither she nor Ernest could tell if they believed them.

Ernest tried to finish the account as briefly as he could. "She told us she knew Sarah would always be loved and taken care of if we kept her. Then, once again, she begged us never to contact anyone in Phoenix about her or the baby. She made us promise that we would not do so. Knowing about her father's drinking problem, it seemed logical to us that she wouldn't want him to know. We thought that she would be afraid of her father." Limply, Ernest finished, "She was so convincing, we believed her."

"And," Carmen said in a broken voice that was almost a whisper. "We wanted to believe her. We wanted Sarah. I begged Ernest to agree that we keep her. Then I was afraid to try to adopt her for fear that somehow, Laura's parents would find out and we'd lose her." She couldn't go on. She put her handkerchief up over her mouth and quietly sobbed. Everyone was quiet.

Ernest finally said, "Carmen, we better go in the kitchen and get dinner on the table."

No one was hungry—they only wanted to talk and ask questions. Each, in their own way, tried to fill in the gap of all those lost years. It was close to seven p.m. before they sat down at the table.

As they bowed their heads in prayer, Ellen realized how very thankful to God she was to have Sarah alive and well. Howard reached over and held her hand. They both felt so much more at peace than when they first arrived. Still, they had so many questions that they wanted answered.

Howard thought, "Why be burdened with questions and answers? We should only be happy and thankful to have our daughter back." Then it struck him. He knew that Ellen had the same thought as her grip on his hand tightened.

Did they have their daughter back?

As they watched Sarah helping Carmen serve the dinner, they knew the answer. Yes, and no.

Yes, she was their daughter by blood, but it was plain to see that she was Ernest and Carmen's daughter. . . by love.

Chapter 17

Monday morning found the Farrells back in Santa Fe at Sheila's house. Over coffee, they avidly talked about all that had happened the day before.

They had arrived back in Santa Fe after eleven p.m., exhausted from the emotions of the day. Steve had driven them back after they finally decided that the twins would join their biological mother and father in Santa Fe. They would visit for a week or more, getting acquainted with each other. It seemed awkward to stay at the Montoya's and everyone agreed that this would be the best for all concerned.

Sarah was reluctant to leave her parents in Velarde and inwardly wondered if they really wanted her to do this without them. It was all decided so fast that this morning as she sat and listened to them rehash the day before, she felt it near to impossible that she was actually here among them. She hardly said a word as they rambled on, for her thoughts and her heart were in Velarde. In her mind, she was seeing her parents sitting at the kitchen table and talking over the events of yesterday.

She was close to tears when she felt Ellen's hand upon her shoulder. "Darling, it's all right. We do not mean to push you. Maybe we made the wrong decision last night about your coming here with us so soon. We were all so tired, it seemed the right thing to do at the time, but now. . . ." Her voice trailed off as she looked at her family for help. Sarah burst into tears and before she realized it, she was in Ellen's arms.

She had a good cry as she felt the warmth of her real mother's love. Without being disloyal to her own parents, she was experiencing a sense of belonging to this family, too. Finally, Sarah was the first to pull away and she smiled at her mother as she wiped her eyes. "I feel much better. Maybe now I can share my thoughts with you instead of just listening to everyone."

Ellen let out an audible sigh of relief as they sat back down. Sarah took a deep breath as she looked at Sheila. She knew that her sister had already anticipated what she was going to say. Since Steve was not here yet this morning, Sarah felt this was as good a time as any to tell them about her life.

They were only a week away from Christmas and so much had happened since last Thursday the fourteenth, when she first found out that she had a twin sister and another family. It seemed like a year and yet it was only five days ago. Still, she felt that things had to keep moving just as fast.

Looking right at her mother, she said, "Ellen, I do not know how to tell you all this except to come right out and say it, being time is so precious and I have very little of it left before I enter the Carmelite Convent."

Silence met this remark, mainly because they were unenlightened as to what she was talking about. All eyes were on her as she went on. "Carmelites are a group of nuns who live together in a convent in order to give glory to God and to pray for priests and for all the people in the world. Their life is one of sacrifice and love"

Sheila interjected here, as she could contain herself no longer. "What she is trying to tell you is that she is planning on locking herself away from the world and from us, because once she enters, she cannot ever come home or be with us again!"

"That's not true, Sheila. You can all come to see me once a month except for the Lenten and Advent seasons." She stopped speaking as she saw the ashen looks on their faces.

Ellen's heart sank as she heard these words and she experienced a feeling of utter devastation in the middle of her stomach. She could not believe what she was hearing. As she looked to her husband for help, she saw that he and Leah both felt the same.

No one knew what to say or do. Although they showed none of the tumultuous emotions Sheila had voiced upon hearing this news, their hearts were torn in two.

Howard moved closer to Ellen and directly across from Sarah. "We are trying to comprehend what you are saying, Sarah, but could you tell us more about this?" As he said this, he gave Sheila a look to be still and let Sarah speak.

"In a few sentences, I could never tell you everything in my heart. As we get to know each other better, you will come to understand, and hopefully, even approve of my life. On January nineteenth, which is only four weeks away, I will enter the convent. This is something that I have given much thought and prayer to. I wanted to enter when I was twenty years old, but the Mother Superior asked me to wait a bit longer.

"At the time, I could not understand this and found it very hard to wait this long. Now, however, with all that has happened this last week, I understand that it was God's holy will, through Mother's decision, so that we would be brought together before I became a nun. I do not want to hurt any of you, but you must realize these plans were already in the making before I even knew of you."

The doorbell rang and Sheila excused herself to go and let Steve in. She opened the door and went right into his arms. "She is telling them now what I told you last night about her entering the convent." Steve stroked her hair and tried to soothe her.

He was glad Sheila had filled him in last night on what had happened since he went to Phoenix to tell the Farrells that they had found Sarah. The two of them walked hand in hand back into the sunroom, where they were met with tension and reserve. A quiet stillness darkened the usually sunny, bright room.

Chapter 18

The sunroom was one of Sheila's favorite places in her home. It was a spacious room with many window-benches and windows looking out at the lovely garden. This was the room where she spent most of her time. Unless she was having a dinner party, she ate her meals in the sun room instead of the formal dining room. This was where she would do her writing and reading. Even now, with the tense silence she could not help feeling that sense of warmth and welcome that came to her every time she entered this room.

Leah brought Steve a cup of coffee as the couple settled down on one of the window seats. Sheila explained she had filled Steve in the night before about everything that was happening.

Ellen started pleading with Sarah not to enter the convent so soon, after they were all finally reunited. Howard made it clear that he could not even tolerate the thought of such a thing, not now and maybe never. Leah confirmed, in an exasperated tone, that she considered the entire thing utter nonsense. She was sure that Sarah could not mean to go through with this preposterous idea, and that it should all be put aside as utter frivolity on her sister's part.

When she was almost finished with her long discourse, Sarah cut her off. "Why can't you understand, or at least be willing to try and understand me, and what I want to do? I imagine that everyone is very happy and understanding about Steve and Sheila getting married!" She wanted to bite her tongue as all eyes turned toward Sheila and it dawned on her that none of them knew this news yet.

Sheila was stunned, but she did not have time to give it much thought. Steve beamed. Leah and Ellen could not hide how happy they were for them, going right up to them with hugs and kisses. Words were flying back and forth.

"When did this happen?"

"We are so happy for you!"

"Congratulations, darling!"

Howard and Sarah looked at each other steadily for a few seconds before Sarah went to Sheila. "I'm sorry, it just came out. I never gave it a thought that they didn't know yet. Everything seems so upside-down right now for all of us. A week ago my life was planned and seemed so simple. Now I am confused as to what I am supposed to do. How am I supposed to feel and act in the midst of all this turmoil among us?"

Ellen rushed from one daughter's side to the other's. "We are all distraught right now; we are so happy to have you back and the thought of losing you again is one I can't bear."

"Well, won't you be losing Sheila too, when they are married, yet you are all so happy over that!"

"It is not the same," Ellen insisted. "We expected this; it was more or less understood they would be married. We won't be losing her; we will be gaining a son. But you will actually be leaving us."

Sarah put her hands up in the air. "Wait, everyone, wait a minute. I can't continue on this way!" Going to the phone, she dialed and waited, as they all watched in anticipation as to what she could possibly be doing.

"Hello, Sister. May I please speak to Mother Mary Gabriel? Yes, it is very important. I need to talk with her." A long pause ensued, then, "Mother, I need to see you today, if it is at all possible. Yes, I am in Santa Fe now and so much has happened in the last five days. I need to tell you all about it. . . I need your help."

Sarah felt a relief as she hung up the phone and turned toward all the eyes that were upon her. "She said I could see her at two-fifteen this afternoon." Turning back to the phone, she dialed home. "Daddy, can you and Mom come to Santa Fe? I need you to be here with me. I need us all to get acquainted together. I can't bear the thought of you both home alone without me."

Listening to Ernest for a few moments, she once again hung up and turned toward all the searching faces. "They are coming," she said as she smiled at them all. "I will try and tell Mother all that has happened and have her meet you, if we have enough time today."

* * * * *

Sarah felt so much better after talking with Mother and knowing her parents would be here sometime late this afternoon. They would stay right here since Sheila's house was so spacious, with four large bedrooms, each having a private bath.

Ellen and Sarah went out into the atrium together. Neither of them spoke for a long time as they walked around, appreciating the scent and beauty of the flowers.

Ellen seemed at a complete loss; she had nothing to say to this young woman who was her daughter. She studied this new-found daughter, with her long hair and dark skin. She was Sheila, but she wasn't Sheila, she was Sarah. Sarah, whom she had missed all through the years. How many times had she looked at her one daughter and seen two, seen Sarah without actually seeing her?

"Sarah, if I could only explain to you. . . I felt such a loss all those years. When Sheila had her first birthday, and every birthday thereafter, I would actually picture the two of you blowing out the candles, opening the gifts, hugging Daddy and me. Sometimes I found myself living in a dream world, you were with us all the time in my mind. When I shopped for Sheila, I dreamed of buying you the same thing. To me it was so real, I would see you holding the dress up and giving me the sweet smile that was so precious to my heart. That same smile was on Sheila's lips. Oh, how can I ever explain? Who could understand, except your father, what I went through and God alone knows what he went through.

"We tried to talk it out so many times as the years went by, but we would always end up in tears, and our emotions were so hard to control. As time went on and special events took place in Sheila's life—her sixteenth birthday, her first date—we were both picturing you with her. We would look at each other, knowing the struggle the other was going through, and then we would bring ourselves back to Sheila and try to subdue the suffering in our hearts."

Sarah's heart was broken as she listened to her mother and saw the pain on Ellen's face. Before she could make any reply, Sheila came out and joined them. Ellen, deep in thought, was still remembering all those times that she had the twins looking the same, dressed the same, playing and talking the same. Her imagination had made them one. Now she realized that, even though they were identical twins, they each had their very own distinct individuality. Coming out of her deep reverie of abstracted musings, she shocked herself as well as both of her daughters when she asked, "Let me see your scotty dogs on your right ankles."

After looking at her for a few moments, they all looked down to see the detailed birthmark on the girls' ankles. There was no doubt that they were identical.

Chapter 19

Sarah sat quietly, listening to Mother Mary Gabriel answer the many questions of her real parents and two sisters.

Mother Mary Gabriel was tall and slender with a serene countenance. She was very dignified in her dark brown habit with the long scapular of brown wool hanging over her shoulders. Her hair and neck were covered. She had a pretty face and beautiful smile that put everyone at ease from the first moment they met her. Her dark eyes were warm and sincere.

Mother had been so calm when, less than an hour ago, Sarah told her all the events of the last week. She had sat in disbelief when she heard how Mother responded to her plea for help. Sarah was reliving in her mind how Mother had told her that she agreed with her family. "My dearest child," Sarah could hear her say. "I understand how very hard this is for you, but I must try and entreat you to do as they say. Give them a year, more or less, as God ordains. It would be utterly impossible for you to enter now, with so many people involved. There is so much to resolve within your own heart, as well as within their hearts."

Sarah took a deep breath and, once again, tried to listen to the conversation around her, but it was no use. She could not help drifting back to Mother's counsel. "Your family lost you so very many years ago. There is no way for them to comprehend they would not be losing you once again when you enter the monastery. God, in His goodness, will take care of all of this in due time. He will have to be the One to render their hearts open to His holy will. You, too, must respond to His will. If they had found you already in the convent, already a novice or a professed nun, it would be entirely different. They would have to accept what they could not change, if that were the will of God. Now, however, a year is very little to give to the family who lost you so many years ago." Mother had deep compassion for Sarah as she told her these things and, as hard as it was, her common sense told her Mother was right. What could she say as Mother told her, "From what you have just told me, you are a very rich woman. Extremely rich. You have not had time to comprehend all that has happened. I agree with your twin sister. Spend time with her and your family. Travel to Europe, as Sheila wants you to do. See what it is like to have everything you want, since you now have the means to do so. Then make your decision about Carmel, based on the fact that you have tried this other way of life, and you have given to your family what they are asking for. Even if they never reach an understanding of our lives or why you still wish to be a nun, God will bless you because of your generosity towards their feelings in this matter."

Go to Europe. Never in her life would she have thought she would have an opportunity to do such a thing! Although she knew she always would have loved to travel and see new places, until now, she had to travel in her mind, through books. In reality, Santa Fe and Taos were the two largest places she had ever gone. She had never even gone to Albuquerque. How many times, as she read of new places, had her heart yearned to see them? Walk the streets, meet the people, sit by the ocean. . . . Deep in her heart, she could not help thinking how exciting it all sounded. But, could she leave Ernest and Carmen, leave Mother, the sisters and the convent, for a year or better. . .?

"Sarah. . . Sarah?" She heard her name as she came back into the parlor. "We are almost ready to leave."

Going to the grille that separated her from Mother Mary Gabriel, she put her hand upon it and Mother's hand instantly came up on the other side and gently rested against hers. Tears glistened in both their eyes as Mother spoke. "Bring your parents—Ernest and Carmen—tomorrow morning and we, too, will have a visit together." Sarah turned toward her new-found family. "Please give Mother and me one more moment together, alone."

As they were leaving, they barely caught the first words she spoke to Mother: "I know you're right, but I don't know how all of this is going to turn out."

Mother's eyes were so full of love as were her words. "We do not have to know the outcome. All we need do is trust and have confidence that our loving Father and Mother Mary will take care of all our needs better than we could ever do. Someday, you will look back on all of this and be happy. One day at a time, Sarah. Remember—one day at a time." With that advice, Sarah backed away from the grille. Her tears ran down her cheeks, oddly accompanied by a beautiful smile. She threw a kiss to Mother and left the parlor.

Mother stood with her hand still pressed to the grille and, as the door closed, so did her eyes. She took a deep breath. Her heart and soul lifted up in prayer. She prayed for this beloved daughter to make the right decisions as the world opened up to her. This new world, which was filled with the unknown and the temptation of the riches at her command. She asked God to bless her and keep her safe. Then putting Sarah in the hands of the Most Holy Mother and St. Michael, she, too, left the parlor.

* * * * *

Ernest and Carmen were so bewildered and confused that Mother Mary Gabriel's heart went out to them, more than ever.

As the four of them visited, she reiterated what she had told Sarah the day before. She encouraged them to trust God and to know that Sarah would always be their precious child.

Sarah listened quietly, remembering how she told her mother and father all of this last night. She had been so happy when they arrived in Ernest's old truck. It was always a worry if the truck would make the trip. She smiled, thinking of how many times they prayed themselves to their destination in that old truck.

Life is so funny, she thought. I can buy them a new truck, now. But how will I go about it? She could hear them now. "No, no, the old truck is just fine." This was all so new to her. She had never had more than a few dollars at one time. They would all strive to save their pennies here and there all year to buy Christmas presents for each other.

I know, she thought. I'll buy them a truck for Christmas. But how do I do that? I still don't have any money. I do not know how to go about asking for it, or how to get it.

When the visit was over, the three of them walked up to the grille. Mother's and Sarah's hands touched once again. "Mother, I trust with all my heart that if God wills it, nothing and no one will keep me from becoming a Carmelite nun."

Mother smiled broadly, showing her pleasure and total belief in the truth of this statement.

Chapter 20

Christmas was spent at Sheila's. She called a nursery and ordered a large tree. Sarah couldn't believe her eyes. Sheila did nothing but give orders and have others come and decorate the tree. She had a housekeeper who cooked for her when she planned dinner parties or special events. That idea was so new to the three Montoyas that their eyes were as big as saucers as they watched what went on around them.

Sarah never mentioned her inheritance to her parents, so a couple of days before Christmas, the three of them went shopping. They climbed into the old truck and went downtown. The day was wonderful, just like old times. They had lunch out together and decided where they would meet when they were done.

Sarah looked at how much she had saved throughout the year. She realized she had a little over two hundred dollars. She couldn't help but laugh out loud as she walked through the store, thinking, "I guess I'll have to buy my father a toy truck. Here I am, an heiress, with no money." Then she got serious. "I have to buy for four more people now, and don't forget Mrs. Ellsbury back in Velarde." The dear old woman had so little, she always liked to get her some fruit and some yarn so she could keep crocheting. Sarah had always loved to visit her and hear the stories of her youth and family.

What can I buy for Steve? After all, he is going to be my brother-in-law. But his was not the most important present. She had planned all year to buy her mother several items. A nice dress, shoes and a purse, a nightdress and especially a robe. Carmen needed one badly and never would buy one for herself. When Sarah had all this shopping done, she looked at how much she had left. "Hmm, a little under one hundred and twenty left." She found a nice shirt for her father. It was so hard to find gifts for the rest. She ended up with a fruit and candy basket for Howard and Ellen, a shirt for Steve, perfume for Leah. Then she looked at blouses for Sheila, and she knew she only had eighteen dollars left. She could not help feeling funny—Sheila wore fifty-dollar blouses, or maybe they even cost more.

Giving up the blouse idea, she was at a loss as to what else she could give her sister. Ending up in a religious store, she finally purchased the Holy Father's book, Crossing the Threshold of Hope, in paperback, and a nice rosary. Not the one she would have liked to buy. . . . She couldn't afford that one.

Christmas Eve dawned, it would be a beautiful day in Santa Fe. The sun was out and it was pretty crisp outside. Sarah was enjoying the garden when Sheila rushed out. She could not hide her excitement as she led her sister through the house to the bedroom. Sheila made Sarah close her eyes as she opened the door. "Now you can open them," she said excitedly.

Sarah gasped as she glanced around the room. There were exquisite dresses and blouses draped over chairs, hanging in the closet, spread on the bed, everywhere she looked. There were shoes and purses, a shawl, a coat. It looked like a clothing store.

"Surprise, surprise!" Sheila was saying. "This is why you have not seen much of me for the last day or two. I hope you like everything."

Sarah did not know what to say. What could she do with all these clothes? How could she possibly wear them all? She held a dress up and tried a pair of shoes on. She couldn't help being happy when she saw how pleased Sheila was. She did not want to hurt her sister by telling her she did not want or need all these clothes. Instead, she hugged her warmly. Pulling away and looking at her happy face, she said simply, "Thank you."

A knock came on the open door and Howard asked, "May I come in and talk?"

The girls sat across from their father. He explained to Sarah that he had opened her accounts in the bank in Phoenix that they used and had her trust fund transferred there. He went on, "It will be two or three weeks before all your money will be available, so I had this deposited in your checking account for now. The rest will be in savings, so whenever you wish to put more in checking, you may do so."

She reached for the checkbook that he was handing her. Opening it, she looked at the amount he had deposited: One hundred thousand dollars. She gasped.

She repeated the amount out loud. Howard said, "You can transfer more from your savings whenever you would like. You actually make good money every month from your interest. If you ever need my help or advice, I will try and guide you."

Sarah looked at him. "Thank you. I don't know what else to say. It does not seem possible that this is happening to me. I do have one question for now, Howard. Could I go out and buy my father a new truck?"

"Honey, you can buy anything you want for yourself, your mother and father, or anyone else. This money is all yours. With all the rest of your inheritance and the interest it has been drawing, you have over a million and a half dollars."

She looked at the checkbook once again, and then looked closer as she saw her name. . . "Sarah Farrell Montoya" and the address was her home in Velarde. She looked at this man who was her real father with a genuine "thank you" in her eyes and expression. Howard understood that the thank you was not for the money, but for the kindness he showed in including the name she always had and the address in Velarde.

At that moment, Sarah knew that these people, her real parents, were good people and her heart became softer toward them.

Christmas morning, Ernest, Carmen, and Sarah rose early to go to Holy Mass. Sheila decided to join them. She couldn't explain why to herself or to anyone else. She only knew she wanted to go. After a lovely breakfast, served in the sun room, they all gathered around the Christmas tree and exchanged presents.

Sarah had decided not to buy any more gifts for the family, but instead to give the gifts that she had already purchased with much thought and love, using the money she had saved all year. She did not add anything to the gifts for the family, not even the truck for her father.

She made one exception without the advice of anyone. She hired a cab and went shopping all by herself, late that Christmas Eve night. She had so much fun. She was like a five-year-old let loose in a candy store. It was amazing to her. She was buying so many items that a clerk followed her into each department, helping her carry her purchases. She picked slippers and a robe and a night-dress for Angela. Then she thought, Why not? I'll buy for her mother and father, too, now that I have the money. I can give them a little something for all the good they have given to me through the years. The dinners at their house, staying overnight with Angela. Taking me along when they went shopping. We had so many good times together.

Then she found a warm coat for Mr. Lewis, who picked up the garbage. She could picture him in it and feel the warmth in her whole body. She could not hide her joy in the gifts she bought as she thought of the people who would receive them.

The sales clerk picked up her excitement and enjoyed helping her find things. "Look, here is a sweater that would make a nice gift." or "How do you like this perfume?" Sarah laughed at that—she couldn't picture old, straight-faced Miss Hernandez using perfume.

"No, for this lady, maybe a blouse. Simple, though. No frills."

They found one gift after another as she checked off her list.

She wrote her first check for three thousand dollars and added a tip for the sales clerk. Then, after having the cab driver drop her off at home, she sent him on to Velarde with a list of names and addresses to make deliveries to.

She smiled as he drove off. His fee, plus the extra she had given him was well worth it. She could visualize the happy faces, the bewilderment when they saw the card: "From someone who loves you."

Chapter 21

January nineteenth, the day Sarah was to have entered the convent, had come and gone.

The Farrells and Sarah had come to Phoenix right after New Year's. The Montoyas went back to Velarde.

It was hard. Sarah was determined to do what Mother suggested and make the best of it.

Now she was restless, having been in Phoenix for four or five weeks. She felt she was wasting time. She longed for the river, walking in it, sitting by it—or even in it. Her home and parents in Velarde seemed so far away. She was experiencing a deep loneliness.

When she arrived in Phoenix, she met her brother, Richard, her sister-in-law, Sue and her nieces, Cynthia and Lisa. They were delightful and she loved them all. Actually, she was learning to love each of the Farrells dearly.

Today after Mass, she sat in silence in the church, thinking and praying. She remembered Christmas back in Santa Fe at Sheila's.

The gifts the Farrells had bought for them were unbelievable. So many gifts. She remembered how embarrassed her mother was. She could still see Carmen's face, how delighted she was with the simple gifts that Sarah had bought with much thought and love.

Carmen told her later, "Sarah, I never saw so many gifts! We didn't bring them any presents, only baked goods and tamales! I felt funny accepting so much."

"Don't worry, they will enjoy all the delicious food you brought and we can't afford what they can," Sarah said. She turned quickly to look at her mother and, flushing, said, "Oh, I forgot. We can afford whatever we want now." Carmen looked uncomfortable. After Christmas, she had told them about her inheritance.

She remembered asking Ernest for advice on all this money. She told him she wanted to buy him a truck, but he would hear none of it. She showed him the amount of money she had and told him about the rest. "Better you than me," he had said. "Be careful, my dearest girl, having money has ruined many more people than the lack of it. Pray, and do not change your standards. Go ahead and enjoy it, along with this time in your life, but be sure you do it with a holy indifference. Otherwise, you will be entangled and caught up in the world and wealth. You will forget the important things in life. Always strive to make the right decisions with honesty, integrity, and sincerity. Family, friends, trust, and love are the important things. Not how much money we have or how much prestige. The wealthiest people who know what the important things are in life, never act like they are better than anyone else."

The more she thought about it, the lonelier she became. She had almost forgotten what her father said. In these few short weeks, her life had changed dramatically. She had her hair cut to match Sheila's, at Ellen's request. She dressed like Sheila. She bought herself a modest car instead of the Rolls Royce Howard wanted her to buy. She sent gifts and money back home and was already depositing more money in her checking account. Only a few weeks ago, she thought she could never spend one hundred thousand dollars in a whole lifetime.

Ernest was not cashing the checks she was sending. Her mother sounded sad on the phone; not happy with the dresses and other gifts she sent.

Their life was so different here. The Farrells meant well, but there were so many dinner parties. There were trips, shopping, the opera, and the theater. Right now, as she pictured Ernest and Carmen back on the farm, she wished she was back there, moving a cow from one pasture to another, or feeding the chickens. Better yet, watching Carmen make tortillas and eating them right off the grill. . . . mmm, she could taste them.

As she entered the house, Ellen met her at the door. Smiling, she reached for her hand. "Darling, you're later than usual this morning."

"Yes, I stayed in church longer. With Sheila back in Santa Fe with Steve this week, I thought there wouldn't be as much to do or as many places to go." Ellen was listening to her as she guided her through the dining room and out into the garden. She could see again how Sarah's spirit seemed so low and she could hardly wait to step out into the garden.

"I have a surprise for you." She needed to say no more, as Sarah saw Ernest and Carmen and ran into their arms. She was so relieved at seeing them. Her joy knew no bounds as she enthusiastically told them all about what she had been doing. Ellen was visibly pleased as Sarah asked Martha to serve lunch on the veranda. Ernest and Carmen's eyes met as they read each other's thoughts.

She has changed so much. Is this Sarah or Sheila talking to us? Their hearts sank; Sarah was no longer herself. She spoke and acted like Sheila. They loved Sheila for her own personality, but they wanted their simple Sarah back.

After lunch, Sarah showed them the house and the grounds. This took a good deal of time because of how vast it was. She then showed them to their rooms and had one of the housemen bring their luggage upstairs. They could not believe that she had a car. Nor could they accept that she already had a license and did not seem afraid to drive around Phoenix.

They felt melancholy and wished they were home where they belonged. To them, life would never be the same again. Even with Sarah entering the monastery, they knew they would not be losing her, but now. . . it seemed as though they really had lost her.

When they were alone, Carmen walked into Ernest's arms. "She has changed so much. She is not our little Sarah anymore." Ernest stroked her hair. His eyes were sad and his thoughts miles away.

"Ernest, I wish we had not let Ellen talk us into coming here. You were right when you said we shouldn't come. I could not stand the thought of Sarah being so sad though, when Ellen explained how she was acting. I thought it best."

Ernest said nothing.

Chapter 22

It did not seem possible to Carmen they had been in Phoenix two weeks already. Here it was almost March first. Where did the time go? It seemed like yesterday when Sheila first knocked on their door in Velarde.

These last two weeks had been very hard, yet the families were coming closer together. They shared so many remembrances of the girls as they were growing up. Ellen and Carmen shared all the little things that they said or did. Ellen had so many pictures to pore over. Ernest and Carmen had none with them and, as a matter of fact, they had very few indeed. They could never afford pictures.

Ernest was biting at the bit to go home. As he told Carmen, "The neighbors have looked after our farm much too long. All our work, along with theirs, is way too much." He was restless and edgy.

Sarah had left a week ago to go back to Santa Fe, to be with Sheila. They were planning a trip to Europe around the first week of April.

Carmen still could not believe that Howard and Ellen talked them into staying here so long. What possible meaning could it have to be here? Everything had been said that could be said. Carmen, who loved to eat out, was sick of all the fancy restaurants. She was ready for homemade frijoles and tortillas. Lost in thought, she did not hear Ellen come out into the garden. She jumped as Ellen sat down and handed her a cup of coffee.

"We need to go home. It was good to come here for Sarah, and you and your husband have been wonderful to us. If I do not get Ernest home soon, I think he will go crazy. He wants to leave tomorrow and so do I. I know you paid to fly us out here to Phoenix, and I do not know how to tell you this, but we do not know how to get home. We just do not have the money." Ellen looked at her in dismay.

"I thought Sarah was sending you checks! Money never crossed my mind!"

Carmen looked sheepish. "She has given us many checks, but we have not cashed them. Ernest does not want the money. Now that you mention it, though, we will do that, so that we can go home." She gave a sigh of relief.

After a pause, Ellen cleared her throat and nervously brought up what was on her mind. "Carmen, I know we both feel a big letdown with the girls gone. We should not have talked you into staying here. It was my thought that we could get to know each other better. Now Howard and I stayed up half the night talking. He is going on a medical trip to New York. He wants me to go with him, but I want to go back to your home with you, if you'll have me for a couple of weeks. I would like to stay in the room Sarah had all these years. See the river she so often talks about, the Rio Grande Gorge, the mountains, and the terrain she loves so much. I want our families to be close. I do not know what else to do in this situation but to try to be like sisters. I would also be close to Santa Fe so we could see our daughters before they go to Europe. Howard agreed we could all drive to Albuquerque. He would fly from there to New York. That way, I would have the car to take you the rest of the way home." She took a deep breath. "We would have to leave early tomorrow morning if we were to do it this way. . . . Would you mind having me at your home?"

"We would love to have you, Ellen. You must realize, however, that there is no way to entertain you at our home as you have done for us here. We hardly ever go anywhere. We do sit on the porch, though, enjoy the outdoors, and listen to records. I do not think I have ever been away from home this long in my life. Nor have I done so many things. I must find Ernest and tell him. He was planning on leaving here in a day or so."

Ellen stood up, smiling. "They are in the garage, looking at all of Howard's tools. Howard is talking to Ernest about this, too. Let's go find them so we can all get packed and ready to go early in the morning."

As they walked out of the room, arm in arm, Ellen spoke softly. "Thank you for coming here. I believe we have become close to each other. I am so happy to be able to come and stay with you now."

Chapter 23

The trip to Velarde had been uneventful. Carmen and Ernest were so happy to finally be home. Ernest resolved not to let this ever happen again.

"Our entire life has changed," he told Carmen. "We've gone on trips, long ones, and put our work on others. I know Sarah wants us to do the impossible, become family, the Farrells and us. This is probably what God would like all people to do, but it's pretty hard to do in real life."

"Yes, Ernest, but this is a complicated situation. Most people wouldn't be called to make this choice. We have to try and all be family because from now on, what involves Sarah will also involve the Farrells. There is no way out. Either we choose to be close to each other or we choose not to. If we make the choice not to, everyone would be unhappy, but it would be Sarah who would suffer the most."

It was as different to Ellen being in New Mexico and living in this new environment as it had been for the Montoyas living in Phoenix. The women ardently talked about the girls. Carmen shared so many stories of Sarah when she was growing up. Ellen couldn't get enough of them. She could listen all day, and still ask Carmen to tell her more in the evening over their late night cup of tea. Long after Ernest retired, the two women would sit and share. A night hardly went by that Ernest's voice didn't boom out, "Carmen, don't you know what time it is? The two of you can talk all day tomorrow." Then he would mumble to himself, "They say the same things over and over anyway. You'd think they would finally get tired of it."

Carmen would sit quietly, smiling. "I'm coming, dear. We won't be much longer." Then for a few minutes, she would try and be still before they were once again engrossed in telling stories.

Now as Carmen looked out the window, she saw Ellen way off in the distance, walking along the river. She felt a twinge of grief; she couldn't help but realize how much Sarah looked like her real mother. They were becoming so close that it no longer seemed strange to have Ellen sleeping in Sarah's room. Ellen had shared with her how she liked to sift through Sarah's belongings. Touching them, holding them close, seeing her daughter's personal belongings meant so much to her. However, everytime anything came up about the monastery or Sarah becoming a nun, Ellen would close herself off from it. She wanted to hear about it and yet she didn't. She didn't even want to be reminded of it. Those were the only tense times between them; otherwise, everything was going smoothly.

Carmen was anxiously looking forward to the girls and Steve coming for dinner on Sunday. She decided she would make a pork roast with homemade dressing and applesauce. It was one of Sarah's favorite meals. How could she know that it was also Sheila's favorite dinner, the one she always asked for on her birthday.

As the mothers shared stories, they realized more than ever how very much alike the girls were. From tiny incidentals to some of their bigger decisions, they would react the same. It was so interesting to hear them share these stories that even Ernest found himself listening attentively as they would reminisce.

Carmen would remember something Sarah did when she was a child or a young adult, and then Ellen would remember a similar situation with Sheila and how she would respond in the same way. From morning until late at night, the women would share. Ellen learned how to peel chile and make tortillas. As she helped Carmen sort beans, she could hardly keep her mind off Howard. He would be here tomorrow. She wanted him to hear everything and share this homey place with her for a few days before they left to go back home. She wanted him to sleep with her in Sarah's bed. To share the room their daughter had all these years. She missed him. This was a healing time for her and she wanted him to have this healing also.

Sunday was a wonderful day. They were all reunited. Dinner was delicious. The girls found it delightful that this was their favorite meal. They, too, had discovered how similar they were in so many areas of their lives. Howard and Ellen felt so good being together in this peaceful valley.

Sheila and Sarah shared all their plans for their forthcoming trip. Sarah was not looking forward to it, but no one could tell.

Sunday evening found Sarah, Carmen, and Ernest sharing their thoughts about Sarah's personal feelings and her inner turmoils. They talked about her deep longing to enter Carmel and start her life as a religious, living for God and for all people, through service in the life of contemplation. Her last words to them before she left to go back to Santa Fe kept coming back to Carmen all evening. "Why can't they respect my decision for my own life? Why can't they try to understand my love for God and His mother? It does not take anything away from my love for all of you. Rather, it enhances my love." She hugged Carmen and Ernest good-bye, wishing it could be different.

Other members of the family were experiencing different senti-ments. Steve was telling Sheila he could hardly stand the thought of her going to Europe and being gone for eight to ten weeks. Sheila confided in him, "Steve, Sarah looks happy and she is really trying to please all of us, but I know how hurt she really is. She is not looking forward to our trip. I feel she needs it, so she will see what she will miss in life if she becomes a nun. I feel torn by my wanting to be with you and to start planning our wedding." With that, she turned toward him and he embraced her tenderly. She would miss him terribly while she was gone.

In Sarah's room, Ellen was showing Howard so many of Sarah's simple possessions. As she tenderly fingered Sarah's Bible, she cried as she thought of losing her daughter all over again.

Chapter 24

Since the first of the year, the months seemed to have flown by. March twenty-first was fast approaching. That was when the two sisters were flying to Europe.

The middle of March found Sarah very restless. Sheila and Steve left early in the morning to spend the day together. Sheila had kept asking her, "Do you mind? Do you mind my being gone all day and evening?"

"No," she felt like screaming. "I don't mind. I want time, I want to think, I want to go home!" These were her inner thoughts as she smiled and assured Sheila that she did not mind at all. She couldn't bring herself to tell her sister how she felt. She did not understand it at all herself.

Now she picked up the phone and tried to offer everything to God and remain calm as she waited to hear the voice on the other end. Finally she breathed a sigh of relief as she heard Mother Mary Gabriel. "Sarah, how good to hear from you! Is everything all right?" Speaking quickly, she asked if Mother might see her this morning. She thanked God when she heard Mother say that she could come right over.

On the way to the monastery, she wondered just what she wanted to say. What did she want Mother to say? It was all so confusing; in a little over a week, she would be on a plane destined for Europe. She knew that Sheila, too, had reservations about going to Europe. Leaving Steve and all the plans for their forthcoming marriage was going to be hard for her. When Sarah had broached this to her, Sheila insisted that they must travel together. Sarah must see all the places she would be missing by shutting herself up in a monastery. Sheila could not accept that Sarah's happiness would be in entering the Carmelite monastery, just as Sheila's was with Steve and their plans for their life together forever.

Sarah was experiencing something new in her life—tension. As she waited for Mother, she felt a knot in her stomach and a tense feeling she had never before experienced. "Why did this have to happen? Why did this family have to come into my life? I would already be in the monastery if they had not entered my life." Then she shook her head as though clearing her mind. "No, no; then I would not have known Sheila, my beloved sister, and my real parents, whom I have learned to love." Her thoughts trailed off as the door opened from the cloister and Mother was there before her.

Rushing to the grille, she put her hand upon it as Mother did from the opposite side. Mother's eyes filled with compassion. Sarah's eyes streamed tears which ran profusely down her cheeks. She could not talk for a few seconds. A feeling of peace was returning to her as she faced Mother. "Sheila is planning her wedding. I want to plan to enter Carmel and be a nun. My real parents and Sheila will not listen to any of my feelings about my life, what I want to do with it. Yet they are ecstatic over Sheila and Steve. Everyone is happy about their plans. I don't even have my own mother and father here with me now to share in my plans." Then with a little laugh, "What plans? My life has come to a standstill. I'm just supposed to be the spoiled rich heiress. . . ." The two women just looked at each other in silence. Then Mother motioned for her to sit down.

"Sarah, all that has happened is so hard on you, yet in all of this, God's blessings are abundant. You must try and get back to living one day at a time. It might be a year or better before this is resolved. In the meantime, you have to be able to go on or you will damage your health. I know you only want what God wills. Have complete trust and confidence in the mercy of Jesus. He is with you and will help you each day. The angels, St. Joseph, and our dearest Mother understand. They are sharing your plans with you. They will help you to know the will of God and bring you to His desired end."

Sarah made no reply. She knew Mother was right, but none of her comforting words helped her at this moment. Mother understood. She needed no response. "Sarah, I wrote down the address of a priest in Rome. He is the brother of Sister Agnes. Sister has written him and told him about you and Sheila, and about your plans to enter our Carmel here in Santa Fe. She has asked him to meet with you, if possible, and give you any help you might need. We will be praying that he will be able to help you in your search for God's will."

Sarah knew as she left the monastery that she had no choice but to go on with her life, day by day, and the plans that everyone else was making for her. This was going to be the only way to reach her true destination, which she felt positive was to be a nun in St. Teresa of Avila's order. And she perceived in her heart that it would be in the Carmel of Santa Fe. Whatever it took to get there, she was willing to do. It didn't matter whether she liked it or not.

So she quietly whispered, as she left the monastery, "Okay, Lord, lead me where Your will takes me. Please lead me back to this monastery, where my heart feels confident You are calling me."

Chapter 25

Steve and Sheila had a wonderful day together. He helped her overcome her apprehension about Sarah. Sheila was so connected to Sarah that she felt painfully sure she was experiencing what was in her sister's heart. The suffering Sarah was going through was heartbreaking, while she herself was at the most happy time of her life. She felt such a deep sorrow as she and Steve started their day, but he would not allow that mood to stay with her. Now, at dinner at the Pink Adobe, one of their favorite places, they were deeply engaged in talking about their wedding plans. They could not set a date with the trip to Europe and the uncertainties ahead.

It had already been decided that they would keep Sheila's house in Santa Fe and make it their home. Sheila was so happy Steve loved the house as much as she did.

Now as she enjoyed dinner, she could not help looking at her engagement ring. "I'm so happy we waited for my ring until the two of us could pick it out together. I love it, Steve, and the wedding bands are perfect for us. Are you as happy as I am about them?" Steve just smiled, showing how pleased he really was. His hand crept over and covered her hand and the ring. He did not have to say a word for Sheila to feel how much he loved her. His hand felt so gentle on hers. His look made her heart quicken and her cheeks flush with joy. "Steve, I can't wait until we are married, until we are one by becoming man and wife. I wish I did not have to go to Europe right now, or ever, as far as that goes."

Steve looked startled. "It is your idea and your family's for you to go to Europe. You know Sarah would give anything not to go. It is because of all of you that she feels pressured into going." Sheila's lip started to quiver, but Steve still went on. "You know it is not the end of the world to become a Carmelite nun. I have lived here all my life and my family has always been in contact with their monastery here. We have asked for prayers and tried to help them with monetary gifts. That is the very least we can do for the many answered prayers and favors they have received for us from God. I remember when my brother had cancer and it did not look like he would make it. The Carmelites stormed heaven for us. My mother went to their chapel to pray almost every day and Mother Mary Gabriel and the sisters helped her very much. The three extern sisters were such a solace to her and our family. She will never forget their prayers and the love she received from them. We believe that God heard their prayers for Paul and healed him completely. Even as little children, we went to Mass at the monastery and became familiar with the nuns. All of us loved our family life together. . . ."

Sheila was visibly agitated as she spoke. "Why didn't you mention how familiar you were with this monastery before this? You let me carry on about it and saw how my family is so upset by this and you still never said anything? How could you do that?"

"What could I say, Sheila? I never really got a chance. When everyone talked about Sarah and the monastery, I knew that what I had to say would not be appreciated, so I said nothing. Now, though, I want you to know my feelings. Sarah has a right to her own life, just as you do. What you can't understand, she understands perfectly and she wishes to give herself to God to be His forever. We, too, need Him as our center, for without Him, no marriage can stay together."

A strange silence came over them both. "My family believes in God but I do not understand how Sarah can give her life. . . ."

"You do not have to understand. Hopefully, someday you will. . . this is not getting us anywhere, Sheila. The main thing is for you both to go on this trip now, to be together, and enjoy each other. Let Sarah be herself. You and I have found a happiness that I am so thankful for. We love each other and want to spend the rest of our lives together. The only thing I am telling you is that Sarah has that same right to be happy doing what she feels led to do with her life. As you share about our plans for our future, the children we hope to have, the years we hope to have together, give her a chance. Let her share and be open to hear what she has to say about her love, her dreams,. . . and her becoming a nun."

Another long silence ensued. Then Sheila reached for Steve's hand again. "I don't understand, but I believe I will be able to, with your help. I hope you will tell me more about your family and your church. It sounds like you enjoyed something very special with your family as you were growing up. My family is close, too, and we love God. You seem to know Him more, though. . . like Sarah does."

It was late when Steve kissed her good night. They had come home and, over coffee, shared a lot more about family, friends, the church, and Sarah. Finally, when Steve left, Sheila felt a lot better about all they had talked about.

Seeing a light still on in Sarah's room, she tapped lightly. "Come in."

Sarah was sitting, reading. Going to her, Sheila curled up in the other chair and frankly told her what Steve had said. Sarah smiled. "I'm better tonight and Mother said the same thing Steve did, that the plans were made, and to go and be together. I believe that, even though both of us now wish we were not taking this trip, for some reason, it is meant to be and God will be with us. I do appreciate knowing Steve believes in my vocation and understands it. Most of all, that he has made you want to understand me."

The two girls stood and hugged each other. Sarah somehow knew that the ice had been broken, as far as Carmel was concerned, and from now on, she could share freely. As she closed her door, she whispered a prayer of thanksgiving and blessed Steve for his part in being the one to finally open Sheila's heart. Even though she knew there would still be obstacles to overcome, it was a beginning. She went to bed feeling better than she had in a long time.

Chapter 26

As the plane took off, both of the twins sat in silence. They were too deeply immersed in their own thoughts to speak. Sarah thought about how Carmen and Ernest had hugged her so tightly. They were not happy about this trip and had made that very clear. She understood how they felt, but she was determined to enjoy this and do all the things Sheila wanted. . . within reason. She missed her parents very much now. As she thought of their life together and how much she loved them, she knew in her heart they would always be her true parents. Their love for her had earned her love. She felt strongly that when love is earned, it always remains true and faithful.

Sheila held her breath so that the sobs she felt within would not escape and be heard by everyone on the plane. Especially Sarah, who was doing this for her. She realized how selfish she had been. She could still feel Steve's kiss and his embrace. She felt the unbearable pangs of loneliness as she had parted from him. Finally, she was able to relate to Sarah's giving up her own desires and dreams for a trip she had never wanted to take.

What utter unselfishness, she thought. How was it all going to work out?

Sheila knew that they must do this to make up for all the lost years. She realized that they must put aside their own longings, their own wants and desires, in order to be able to enjoy this holiday together. This was March twenty-first; they would be coming home May seventeenth. Her heart kept crying inwardly. This must be a good time for us together. I must put aside my own unhappiness. "Sarah," she said. "Please forgive me for pushing this trip on you, for insisting we go and how good it was going to be. Right now, all

I can do is hope it will be good. I feel devastated and betrayed by my own self for forcing you—for forcing both of us—into this."

Sarah reached over and squeezed her hand, letting her know that everything would be all right. Her sweet smile and the pressure on her hand brought peace to Sheila. She was able to breathe deeper without feeling she would fall apart.

The families watched the plane disappear on the horizon. Steve longed for Sheila to be with him. He reminded himself that two months was only eight weeks; somehow it seemed easier to think of it that way.

They all left the airport deep in their own thoughts. The Montoyas went back to Velarde. There seemed to be nothing to say. Steve headed back to Santa Fe and the Farrells started back to Phoenix. It had been a wonderful time for them in Velarde with Ernest and Carmen. It seemed a miracle how the families had knitted together. Their daughters had brought them close. They knew they had formed a closeness that could not be described, only lived.

Ellen felt different now that she had spent time in Velarde with Carmen. The sharing about the girls, the living in Sarah's room and seeing where she was raised helped her to cope with losing her daughter, finding her, only then to realize that she was not actually their daughter anymore. All through the years, she had thought of Sarah as their daughter; now she thought of her as someone else's daughter. All those years she actually was not theirs, but the Montoyas' daughter. It was strange, but now she could cope with it, even understand it. Something that seemed impossible to her was possible, not through human means, but through the divine help and providence that was coming to them all. How many times had she heard Sarah say similar things. Now, though beyond her understanding, she was experiencing that peace that comes from God. She looked at her husband. He, too, seemed peaceful. She decided to bask in the peace of the moment and say nothing.

Instead, she let her hand slide into his, and felt his love and warmth as he turned and looked lovingly into her eyes.

Chapter 27

They had a wonderful time in Europe. In most of the countries, they only had two or three days because it had been planned that Rome would be where they would spend the better part of their trip.

They enjoyed each day to the fullest. To satisfy Sheila, they stayed at the most elegant hotels and dined in the most elite restaurants where the food was delicious but very rich. Sarah would sometimes think, Oh, what I'd give for a bowl of beans and some homemade tortillas, as she watched Sheila eating myriad plates of shellfish.

To satisfy Sarah, they went to the shrines at Lourdes and Fatima, where she prayed so fervently for her family—the ones she had always known and loved and now for her extended family whom God had brought back into her life. She put herself and both families into the hands of Our Lady.

Sheila was very thoughtful and sober while visiting the shrines. She knelt next to Sarah and wondered, How can I persuade her not to enter a convent? I hope this trip makes her see what she would be missing.

Sheila loved all the flamboyancy. Sarah, on the other hand, felt touched by the hand of God in the depth of her soul as she took in the beauty of the river and the gorges. She felt deeply the emotions of love, joy, loneliness, and sadness. Yet, the exhilaration and praise of God's great majesty and goodness in His created universe was part of her perception, too.

She took a deep breath as she thought of their trip so far. She, too, had her way in many things. She had found her way to the best cathedrals, such as Notre Dame de Paris. She had thrilled to being there in the morning, and again at sunset, to see the great cathedral's image reflected in the Seine.

They had a slight conflict of interests as they visited the different places. Sarah getting her way in going to some of the cathedrals and village churches, and Sheila pulling her sister into the boutiques, the restaurants and, of course, the theater. All of this kept their days and nights filled. Sheila kept saying, "We can sleep later. Now, let's do all we can together."

Sarah had to admit it was a good time. They were enjoying themselves immensely.

Then it was on to Italy, the last stop being Rome before departing for the United States.

Sheila was used to having a car and driver to drive them around Europe. Sarah finally talked her into biking in the outlying villages of Tuscany. It took longer for Sheila to get used to a bicycle, especially in some of the high traffic areas, than it did for Sarah when she bought her car and received her license in Phoenix. They both enjoyed the many laughs and frustrations of their bicycle trips, despite getting lost a few times. Sheila had never bothered much with a bicycle when growing up. This had always been Sarah's mode of transportation if she wanted to go anywhere. They started bicycling everywhere they went.

The bicycle outings were a part of their trip that neither of them would ever forget, even when a tire would go flat, or bike break down. Then Sheila's patience would wither. Sarah would experience a deep inner stress until she would hear her sister speak fluent Italian and get them out of the situation.

One day, two young men asked to join them for bicycling and then for lunch. They declined. On other occasions, when men would show any interest in them, their demeanor made it known that they were already taken. They had no interest in male companionship. The two were in Europe to make up for so many years of separation. This they did. Their days were filled with sight-seeing and their nights with sharing their memories of the past twenty-two years.

Finally, they arrived in Rome. . . right in the heart of Rome. They would stay in a simple and prayerful convent. This had been decided, long before, as Sarah had given in on most everything in all the other places they stayed. She had her way a few times, with the bicycling and visits to the churches, but most of the time, Sheila directed the daily plans.

Rome was hers. They would stay where she wanted, at the convent. They would eat there and rest. She would have prayer time. Time to think and meditate. She wanted to see the outside of St. Peter's, even before they went to the monastery.

At the convent, the tables were turned. It was Sheila who felt uncomfortable, who did not know what to do or how to act. This was a first for Sheila. Since she had been seven years old, the world seemed to be hers to command. Once again, her fluent Italian was a help, speaking to the sisters at the convent. Sarah said a devout prayer of thanksgiving for this, and asked God to bless their visit to His Eternal City of Rome. Little did she know that the hand of Divine Providence had already taken care of her prayers.

Chapter 28

Sarah, in her deepest imagination, never thought she would ever go to Rome.

Rome. . . . She would take it with her, in her heart, right into Carmel. Her very being was enthralled at being here. Vatican City, the center of the Catholic Faith. Rome and the Vatican were always alive in her heart, but now she was on fire with love and awe at the beauty of St. Peter's Basilica and St. Peter's square.

She breathed a prayer of thanksgiving to God that she had the confidence to tell her sister, "I have done all you wanted me to do for the last five weeks or more. This last three weeks in Rome, it is your turn to do what I want. Please try and understand my way of life." She knew Sheila felt uncomfortable, and she loved her more than ever when Sheila was willing to do this for her. It would be such a different way of life for her, but Sarah was determined she would help her all she could. She felt deep within that they would both be all the better for their stay here in Rome and in the convent.

As they entered the small, cozy room on the fifth floor, Sheila couldn't help feeling better, even though she wondered where in the world she was going to put all her clothes and all the things she had bought on their travels. She was completely amazed when the cab driver only brought in two small traveling bags. One for her and one for Sarah. She turned quickly toward her sister. "Don't be alarmed, Sheila. Remember, you promised to do what I want here. I had all your purchases and most of your belongings sent home. We will both live with one bag of clothing and a few needed articles for the rest of our trip."

"How could you presume to do such. . .?!"

Sheila never could finish her sentence, as Sarah embraced her and reminded her, "You promised."

"I did," she admitted. "This is your piece of cake."

They went out on the balcony and looked at the city. As they turned to the left, there loomed St. Peter's. They sat out for awhile in silence, then freshened up to go down for dinner. The elevator took them to the first floor where they disembarked and walked across to the small dining room reserved for guests. The sister smiled as they entered and showed them to their table. This would be the table they would have for their entire stay. There were other guests, sitting, quietly conversing, at their tables. Sheila was decidedly uncomfortable and felt better when she saw that Sarah did not know the routine, either. They were halfway through the simple meal before they started to feel at ease with the surroundings and with each other. Everything was so clean and plain and quiet. The table was set for two with a pitcher of water and two glasses and a basket of bread. Sister first brought them a small platter of salad with oil and vinegar. Then they had roasted chicken with some peas, then fruit. That was it.

Sheila had to admit there was something about how the food was cooked and served, and something about the atmosphere of the room that made it special, almost elegant, in the midst of simplicity and humble surroundings.

"I have to say, Sarah, this is very different, but pleasant. The sisters are so friendly and cordial. The food is prepared so well, it really is delicious. I never would have believed I would be staying in a convent in Rome. Ever since I found out about you, my life has not been the same."

Sarah laughed. "If you think your life has been changed, you ought to be me! I was a poor farm girl. I thought I knew what the future held for me. I never traveled or went anywhere far from home. We rarely went out to eat. I drove the truck on the farm, but never took the time to go get my license. My wardrobe was very skimpy. I could go on and on. Now I have more money than I ever thought possible, my own car, more clothes than I can wear in a life-time. I've dined out at the finest places and here I am in Rome, the heart of the Church. The one place I've always dreamed of seeing. You never know what God is going to do next when you're open to His will." She paused. "Do not take this in the wrong way or think I do not appreciate everything. I'm forever thankful that I have you for a sister. We are so different and yet so much alike. I've loved being with you. . . but my heart still yearns to enter the monastery. Being together on this trip will be a treasure in my memory all of my life. No one will ever be able to take it away from me. You have been able to go on with your plans, though. You and Steve have talked so many times together, although you are so many miles away. I feel like I have been cut off from everything I've had before, especially the simplicity of my life. I felt confident that I knew what I wanted and now I can only pray and hope."

She stopped abruptly and they finished their dinner in silence. It was a silence that Sarah cherished, but made Sheila uncomfortable. They looked at each other and understood. They said grace and left the dining room, discussing their plans for tomorrow.

During the next few days, they went to the catacombs, the Christian burial grounds of the early martyrs, where the neat shelves that cut into the rock housed the dead. They went to the Pantheon, to all the major churches—St. Mary Major, St. Paul outside the walls, St. John Lateran. All but St. Peter's. Sarah had called Father William and he was going to go with them and give them a guided tour of St. Peter's, starting with Mass at seven a.m. in the Petrian Chapel. He also got them on a tour of the Scala Regia and a pass to see the Vatican Gardens. They went to Assisi, Loretto, Orvieto, San Domenico, St. Maria Goretti, and the Coliseum.

Something strange was happening to Sheila. She did not dare to think of it or say anything to Sarah. As she went to Holy Mass every day with her sister and watched as Sarah approached the altar to receive Jesus, she felt a strong, deep desire to be able to have Him come to her, too. She was starting to see Rome and the Church through Sarah's eyes. She was as excited as Sarah when they toured St. Peter's with Father. It was a long and exhausting day for her, though a wonderful one. She had so very many questions. He patiently answered them to her satisfaction. At the end of the day, to the surprise of both Sarah and Father, she asked if they would be able to visit with him again so she could have more answers to the questions that kept coming to her.

It was arranged and Sheila learned about Catholicism, about what Catholics believe. It was so different from what she thought. Each morning, in Mass, her desire grew deeper to receive Jesus. It was as if He, Himself, was calling her and wanting her to come forward. Things were happening too fast for her. Every question she had concerning the faith was answered to her complete satisfaction and she did not seem to need deep dogmatic teachings to be able to comprehend it. Her faith was coming alive. She devoured books well into the night. Long after Sarah was asleep, she was up reading and it was more than once that Sarah would open her eyes in the middle of the night and see her sister on her knees, deep in prayer. She never said a thing; she only closed her eyes and prayed.

May seventeenth approached fast. In two days, they would be leaving for home. Sheila had been going through one of the deepest turmoils of her life. In fact, other than finding out she had a twin sister, she had lived a sheltered life of ease and comfort. She loved God, she went to Church with her parents when they went. When she moved to Santa Fe, she went on and off, when her spirit moved her. Then, when she met Steve, she went to Holy Mass with him several times. Now all she could think of was that she wanted desperately to become a Catholic. She saw things so differently now. She wanted to be one with Steve completely. To believe the same as he did and to raise their children Catholic.

Father William helped her understand Sarah's vocation. He compared it to her wanting to marry Steve, to be a wife and a mother. This was her vocation. She never thought of marriage as a "vocation". As having a duty to her husband and children that must be fulfilled. That first and most of all her marriage would be God-centered—"a vocation from God". It wouldn't be just her and Steve. It would be God, Steve, and her. Father told her so many things that she would never have thought of on her own.

This morning, she sat on the balcony looking at St. Peter's dome. Sarah came out and sat next to her. Neither of them spoke for a long time. "Sarah, I do not know how to say this, except just simply to say it. I want to become a Catholic. I want to receive Jesus. To love His mother as you do. The fact is, I do love her, I love Him deeply, and I love the Church. This has all happened so fast, yet I feel completely sure of myself. Father William put me in touch with Father George, who has been giving me instructions and I have studied and read well into the night. I feel so strongly that God wants me. He has given me a calling just as he has given you."

They just stared at each other for a few minutes and then as she realized what Sarah was thinking. "Oh, no, not that far! I do not want the vocation of being a Carmelite nun, but now, I do understand your vocation." Reaching over for Sarah's hand and looking deeply into her eyes, she said, "I do understand now what I firmly believed I would never understand. God has blessed me with the gift of faith and understanding in a very short time. He has showed me we do not need long when we have faith and when our heart is open to the truth."

Sarah was overjoyed. She had believed in her heart that this was happening to her sister, but she had kept quiet and let God do whatever He was doing. Now her heart sang songs of praise. The two sisters stood on the balcony of the convent, staring off at St. Peter's. Then as one, they turned toward each other and in the shadow of the dome, they embraced as they felt their oneness being enveloped by the almighty hand of God.

It was a moment neither would ever forget.

Chapter 29

The first thing the two sisters did after breakfast was call Father William. Sheila told him over the phone everything that she had told Sarah. Father was exuberant over her decision, as he was able to see how the Lord was leading her. He had been praying for her to see and know God's holy will. The next call was to Steve.

This call Sheila made alone. "Steve, darling, I love you and I want you to know first, even before I call Dad and Mom. . . ." She took a deep breath. "Steve, I am going to become a Catholic." From then on, the excitement kept building as she shared her feelings, doubts, and faith. She talked about the many emotions, tears, and prayers, that she had been going through for the last three weeks. "Steve, I don't want to come home right now. Sarah does not know this yet. I want to stay in Rome at least another month, and enter the church here, right in the chapel of St. Peter's."

"Darling, that sounds wonderful, but what do you think your parents are going to say about all this, especially when they are expecting to see you both in only two days? And what about me? I can't wait to have you home to hold you in my arms and tell you once more how much I love you."

"Steve, wait, that is what I want to talk to you about. Please help me work this out. I want you to come to Rome the week I am going to enter the church. I want Dad and Mom here and all of the family, if they can come—Richard, Sue, the girls, and Leah. I want you here with me as I take one of the most momentous moments of my life, this great gift that God has given me must be shared by all those I love so dearly. Even if they do not come, Steve, I need to know that you will."

"Of course, I will, darling. . . ." Before he could finish, Sheila went on.

"Then please work it all out with the family and get them here, too. I am going to call them when I hang up. They will need you to help them understand my decision. I am counting on your wisdom to answer their questions and to put their minds at ease." They continued their conversation, trying to work out the details as best they could.

Over lunch, Sheila told Sarah all about her phone call and Steve's reactions. Then both faced the fact that it was time to call their parents. They were well aware that the weeks were going to fly by.

"Sheila, before you call Howard and Ellen, I must confess to the thoughts and desires that have come to me ever since you told me your plans this morning. I want to enter the monastery as soon as we go home."

"Sarah, let us take this one gift that God has given us—my entering the church—and enjoy all He gives us through this, one moment at a time. Then when we get back to the states, you can plan your entrance into the monastery and I will plan my wedding."

"You're right, Sheila. I'm sorry I brought this up right now."

Ellen picked up the phone. She was ecstatic when she heard Sheila's voice.

"Darling, we can't wait to see you both, the entire family is going to be at the airport. We are arranging for Ernest and Carmen to come over during the week. . . ."

"Mother, Mother, wait! Let me tell you something."

Ellen paused and she seemed to sense that she needed to prepare herself for what she was going to hear.

"Mother, please don't be too disappointed because I want to stay in Rome for another three or four weeks. Well, for however long I need to stay to become a. . . Mother, I don't know exactly how to tell you this and there is no way to explain it. Is Daddy there? Oh, well, you will have to tell him then, because I am just bursting with the good news I have to tell you. Mother,. . . I am going to enter the Church. I am going to become a Catholic. . . . Please, do not say that, Mother; it is not a quick decision. It is something that the Lord is doing in my heart and soul."

Sarah listened, and quietly prayed, as she watched the different expressions cross her sister's face and heard her words. She realized, more than ever, how the two of them were one in so many ways. She was feeling and experiencing emotions in the depth of her soul, and she knew they were exactly what Sheila was feeling. Finally, it was her turn and she took a deep breath as Sheila handed her the phone.

"Hello, Ellen. No, I really didn't talk her into it. I didn't even talk it over with her, although I could see it happening, even before our trip."

Now, it was Sheila looking at Sarah, anticipating her words and actions, and feeling their oneness in the extreme of her very being. She reached for Sarah's hand. They looked peacefully into each other's eyes as they held hands and took turns talking to Ellen and trying to answer her questions.

An hour later, the phone rang in their room. Sheila answered. "Hello, Daddy. I guess Mom explained everything to you. . . . Well, I can't explain it any better. You will have to trust me when I tell you I know and believe it is God's will."

After talking for almost another hour, it was arranged that Howard would cancel their reservations for May seventeenth and leave the departure date open until further notice. Sheila also asked him to call Steve and let him answer any other questions they might have.

It was a full day of phone calls as Sarah finally heard her mother's voice. "Mom, oh, how much I miss you and Daddy! Mom, I have some wonderful news, but first, I must tell you—we are not coming home this week. We will be in Rome another three or four weeks. Mom, I already called Mother Mary Gabriel and told her the news. Sheila is coming into the church right here in Rome!"

"Oh, Sarah, what a blessing! When did this all happen?" Carmen was so sincerely happy, Sarah wished she could put her arms around her and give her a big hug right now.

"Mom, we will share all of that when you get here. The rest of the family is coming to Rome and I want you and Dad to come also." She listened patiently for a few moments. "Mom, you do not need any money and, even if you did, you could cash all of those checks you are hoarding, the ones that I have sent you every month. Please, Mom, never mind all that. I need you and Dad to come over here with Steve and the Farrells. It is very important for both me and Sheila that you be here for this. Steve is going to contact you with all the details. Right now, we are hoping for somewhere between June fifth and July first. We have to see what the priest who has been giving Sheila instructions the last few weeks decides. Mom, please stop interrupting me, I will not take 'no' for an answer, and tell Dad that, too. If you want to make me happy before I enter Carmel, you will come to Rome with the Farrells because, more than anything else in the world, I want you and Daddy to see Rome, to enter St. Peter's and touch the foot of his bronze statue. You must see how the love and touch of the faithful have worn down the bronze on the foot of this majestic work of art. . . . Mom, I don't care how you tell Dad or how you get him to come, just do it! For me." She smiled, knowing that somehow Carmen would convince her father.

Finally, the two sisters who had been separated for so many years, some might say by fate, others by the hand of God, embraced once again, as they had early this morning on the balcony.

Sarah pulled away and, looking into her sister's eyes, said, "It has been a long, hard day, but, oh, what a glorious one!"

Sheila just smiled and nodded her head in perfect agreement.

Chapter 30

Sheila had already been baptized, so it was arranged that she would make her Profession of Faith, receive Jesus in Holy Communion, and be confirmed on June fifth.

On Sunday, June first, they waited anxiously at the airport for their parents' flight to get in. They were all coming together. The two girls were beside themselves with joy and happiness at their expectations of being reunited with the family.

Sheila saw Steve immediately and ran into his arms. He held her close and did not want to let her go. The two of them were in complete oblivion about what was happening to the rest of the family. Sarah embraced Ernest and Carmen, finally pulling herself away so she could embrace Howard and Ellen, then the hugs ensued with Cynthia and Lisa, Richard and Sue, and Leah. Everyone was talking at once and the excitement was high. Sheila finally pulled herself away from Steve and went from one to the other, embracing them.

Sheila shared with them all that God was doing in her life and how she came to her final decision. Yes. . . to the amazement of Ellen and Leah, as well as the rest of the family, they were all staying at the convent in Rome. At dinner, they talked and shared quietly at a much larger table than the girls had had. Later, they all settled in their own rooms.

It had taken some doing on Sheila's part to get them all to stay here, but she was determined and the Mother Superior worked with her on arranging the details. They put cots for the little girls in Richard and Sue's room, which made it very crowded, but workable. Most of the rooms were filled with other guests so they had to make do the best they could. Leah stayed on a cot with her sisters.

Howard and Ellen had their own room, as well as Ernest and Carmen, and, at the last minute, a room became available for Steve.

Sheila asked the sister to put wine as well as water on the tables this evening and the families were all relaxed and enjoying being together. They loved hearing about all the experiences the girls had on their trip. They shared many laughs and tears as they listened to the girls' stories, especially about Sheila riding a bike.

"Picture me trying to keep up with her!" she grimaced as she pointed at Sarah. "Come to think of it now, though, I was really starting to feel like a pro!" The girls looked at each other and laughed.

They reminisced about all they did together on this trip. What a blessing it was. Sarah had to admit, "I did not want to come to Europe, but now, I am so happy I did not stand in the way of God's will, and I'm thankful for the guidance I received from Mother."

Once in their own room, Ellen turned to Howard. "How can life be explained? Who would have thought that you and I would be staying in a convent in Rome? Every once in a while, I feel like I am going to wake up. Howard, I do not understand my feelings. I am actually happy to be here, and to be reunited with our daughters. To see how happy Sheila and Steve are. And most of all, I feel Ernest and Carmen have always been a part of our family." As she ended on this note, she had a look of bewilderment on her face.

Howard reached over and put his hand on top of hers. "I feel the same," he said with great emotion in his voice. "My dearest wife, I feel the same," he repeated, as their cheeks came together and, for a moment, they felt like time had stopped and was waiting for them to catch up with it.

On June fifth, Sheila received Jesus for the first time in Holy Communion. It was more than she anticipated, more than she expected or thought possible. As He came to her, she actually knew and felt His Presence within her. It was overwhelming. She basked in it, and did not want to leave the church after Mass was over. Everyone else waited for them as Steve, Sheila, and Sarah knelt and thanked God silently before joining them outside the chapel.

The rest of the day was spent in thanksgiving and feasting. They all had dinner with Father William and Father George at the seminary. The food was deliciously prepared by one of the brothers, and the other brothers served it. The Farrells and the Montoyas were given a tour of the grounds. All in all, it was a wonderful day.

At nine-thirty p.m., a knock came on Howard and Ellen's door. They were sitting out on the balcony. Howard opened the door.

"May I come in and talk to you?"

"Please do, Sarah. We are on the balcony. Would you like to join us there?" She nodded and followed him, waiting as he found a chair for her to sit on.

"I need to tell you something before we all leave to go back home. I want you both to know I have come to love you very much." She could not go on, as Ellen tried to stifle her sobs. Howard went to her, putting his hands gently on her shoulders. Sarah, too, went and knelt on the floor in front of her mother's chair, putting her hands into Ellen's. "I know how much you must have suffered all these years and yet, I was safe, I was loved, I was alive. I'm sure sometimes you thought I was dead, or hurt, or in an unloving home. Instead, I was given to a family who loved me as their very own, and I loved them and have been very happy. That is why you must try and understand—to me, they are my very own parents whom I shall always love and cherish. That does not mean that I am not your daughter, too. I am. And now that I know you both, I love you."

They all stood at this time and hugged each other as it was hard to speak. They stood in a circle, arms entwined, and let the tears flow. In a few moments, they separated. Howard handed Sarah his handkerchief and stepped into the room to get himself one and blow his nose. When he came back out on the balcony, Sarah went on, "I want to thank you for loving me so much that you have been able to understand and accept my father and mother as part of the family. That is what I want and I ask you to continue to do so when I enter the convent. I want you all for my family. I want to know you will always be close. In a world where some people look down on the family, I want you all to be a shining example of God's love, and show that real love can overcome all obstacles. It may seem that I want the impossible, but it is evident that God has put His hand of Divine Providence on us. We found each other and, although my parents' background and mine are so different from yours, it has made no difference to you. You have treated us as equals. I have seen this and I appreciate it from the depths of my heart, as I know my parents do. You have acted with so much dignity and strength of character over Sheila becoming a Catholic, and I want you to know I love you for it."

She reached up and kissed Howard on the cheek. "Thank you, Father, for loving me so much." Then turning to Ellen and looking her straight in the eyes. "Thank you, Mother, for loving me so much that you love Ernest and Carmen with me and for me, and that you understand they will always be my parents, the same as you are."

All Ellen could do by this time was hold her close while stroking her hair and saying, "Sarah, our dear Sarah, thank you for calling us Father and Mother. Even if you never say it again, you said it once. Thank you for that."

Chapter 31

They had been home for over a week now, and Sarah knew that God was preparing her path into Carmel. Everything seemed to be moving swiftly toward this goal. She could feel it in the very depth of her soul.

When they arrived at the airport in Albuquerque, it had already been decided that she would go back to Santa Fe and continue to stay with Sheila. Now, however, she felt deeply moved to go back to Velarde and her beloved home and parents.

She needed time. Time to prepare herself mentally and spiritually for her entrance into Carmel. She could picture her room and the river, Carmen in the kitchen preparing tortillas, she even imagined she smelled the beans and the chile colorado. . . .

Sheila and Steve were planning their wedding, getting the invitations, everything was falling into place, except for the date. An idea had been forming in Sarah's mind ever since Sheila first told her she wanted to become a Catholic. An idea she wanted more time to think and pray about. She felt confident that if she went home by her beloved river, God would help her put all the pieces together.

At dinner, she broached the subject. "Sheila, I am going home to Velarde to be with my parents and prepare myself to enter Carmel. I'm glad that we decided to spend this evening together tonight. I have been wanting to talk over with you some of the sentiments that have been occurring to me. They have been happening in such a manner that I believe it is God leading me."

"What kind of sentiments? You look excited and have a distinct bearing in your eyes and manner that tells me something is brewing in that beautiful head of yours."

Sarah smiled, showing her inner pleasure and anticipation. She leaned closer to Sheila as though someone else might hear what she only wanted her sister to hear at this time. "I want to enter Carmel on our birthday—August twenty-fourth. I want to go home to think and pray about this, because an idea has been forming in my mind." She took a deep breath. "Sheila, why couldn't you and Steve be married on August twenty-fourth at Carmel? I could be at your wedding. You and all the family would be present to see me enter the monastery and embark on my journey to God and be His forever. It could be a double celebration."

Sheila looked aghast. "Sarah, how could you think of doing such a thing?! Everyone would be so happy about my wedding and so. . . ."

Sarah jumped up from the table and walked to her room as fast as she could. She was shutting the door, when, "Sarah, wait! Let me in! What is the matter with you?"

Sarah turned quickly and for the first time, Sheila could see anger along with hurt and a real sorrow in her sister's eyes and voice. ""No, not what is the matter with me! No, no, no, not what is the matter with me, what is the matter with all of you? It is all right for you to be happy, for you to marry Steve. To go off and do what the two of you want and be happy ever after, that is fine! Right! But I'm not supposed to do what makes me happy, to do with my life what I want to do! Did you get permission from me to marry Steve? If I say I don't want you to get married, is that going to stop you? Sheila, I should not have told you my idea. I needed to pray more about it first and that is what I am going to do at home in Velarde!"

Sheila watched as her sister pulled her suitcase out of the closet and, during this outburst, started packing her clothes. She never saw Sarah so upset. "Please, please, wait." She put her hands on her sister's shoulders and turned her toward her. "Wait. I was wrong to react as I did. You are right; it is your happiness we are talking about, as well as mine. Let's have the rest of this evening together as we planned. Please give me another chance to hear this idea of yours."

They both stood quietly, looking at each other and Sarah could feel the tenseness leaving her and Sheila could feel the anxiety leaving her. Now it was Sheila who smiled. "Who could ever believe that I am starting to get excited over this idea?

"Come, Sarah," she said as she pulled her sister toward the door. "Come, we will spend the rest of this evening talking this over and making plans together for our future happiness." They both hugged tightly before turning and walking, arm in arm, toward the sun parlor.

They sat on the floor and planned well into the night. The later it got, the more excited they were. When they finally went to bed, neither sister could sleep. As Sarah lay wide awake, a knock came and the door opened slowly.

"Are you awake?" Sheila whispered. "I can't sleep and I thought of a few more good ideas."

Sarah smiled and thanked God.

Chapter 32

Preparations were well under way. Going home to Velarde had proved so fruitful. Sarah spent days and early evenings by the river, walking and singing, sitting and reading. This time of solitude did so much for her soul.

Sitting on the porch in the evenings with Ernest and Carmen, the sharing, laughing, and talking would always be remembered deep in her heart. She knew how much it would always mean to them. She could not help but thank God for changing Sheila's mind and opening her heart. Sheila really wanted her wedding day to be on Sarah's entrance day, on their twenty-third birthday.

Sitting by the river this morning, she smiled as she remembered how all the family took the news. All of them had different reactions, but one by one, they came around when they saw how much Sheila and Sarah both wanted it this way. Being united together in their decision made it easier for everyone. Steve was overjoyed right from the beginning. He really liked the idea and helped them with all the details.

Mother Mary Gabriel gave permission for the date Sarah would enter, but was uneasy and hesitated on the wedding taking place in the chapel. This was something that was usually not allowed. After much prayer and talking with the cloistered nuns, it was finally decided that these seemed to be exceptional circumstances, considering all that had happened in the case of the two sisters. Sarah would never forget how the three of them waited to receive Mother's decision.

The excitement ran high in the parlor that day as Mother smiled at them from behind the grille and nodded her head yes. They practically jumped for joy. Steve kissed Sheila, Sheila kissed Sarah, everyone hugged, and Sarah walked to the grille and placed her hand upon Mother's and silently said "Thank you."

Her heart sang: "Taste and see the goodness of the Lord."

Chapter 33

With time running out, Sarah realized how many decisions she had to make. She had been thinking for so long about all the good people she knew here in Velarde, how many were suffering and had real needs that she could help alleviate. So many of them needed temporal help and she had the means to help them.

This morning, she sat by the river with her pad and paper. There was consternation written all over her face as she listed names and ideas of how to help these people.

The Sanders family, for instance. One thing after another had befallen them. Now she could lighten their troubles and they, in turn, could make her so happy by accepting help. Even though they would not actually know it was from her, most of them would guess. The thing was to get them to realize that God provides and they should accept. That, in turn, is the gift they give back to their benefactor. After all, what she had was given to her by God to use for His honor and glory.

With this is mind, she went back to the Sanders family and wrote in her notebook, "New roof and complete renovation of their house. Hospital bills paid in full." Howard would have to work out the details with the lawyer. She would let them know what she wanted done.

Then there was the Garcia family. Their mortgage on the store needed to be paid in full so they would not be under such stress. They helped the community so much. How often had she heard them tell people, "Don't worry about it; pay us next week or as soon as you are able"? Yes, the Garcias would be helped in their small business.

Then there was old Mrs. Flute. She must be given every comfort. She had always loved the children so much. She had so little, but she was so happy.

As she sat and thought about her neighbors and friends, her list kept getting longer and longer. She did not want to forget anyone. Name after name was added and a short summary of the help to be provided.

Then there was her father and mother. The house must be completely paid for, and they could use new tools to make their life easier. Cattle too. . . her pen raced across the paper as she thought of one thing after another for her own family.

Sarah thought Angela and her family could not be forgotten. Then her parish church and Father—a large donation there. She wanted to help the Carmelite monastery. All through the years, these sisters aided and helped the community, as well as the world, by their sacrifices and prayers. Then there was the Legionaries of Christ. She wanted to give them a large donation. Their order was growing and she knew they could use the financial assistance.

Before she finished, she added her one last request and smiled as she wrote it out. No one else would know about this one until August twenty-fourth and she would take care of it herself. She laughed out loud as she relished the idea and pictured the details. The thought of this last bequest gave her immense joy and pleasure, even to the point of wishing to be there to see the outcome. Instead, she would be settled in her new home and she would take pleasure in sharing this one thing with her new sisters in Carmel.

Picking up her notebook, she laughed all the way back to the house and could hardly contain herself for the rest of the evening. This one thing gave her more pleasure than anything else.

Chapter 34

"Are you sure you want to do this, Sarah? Why not wait two or three years or longer until you are professed and then you could renounce all your possessions. . . ."

"Howard, please help me, as you promised. What you do not understand is that once I enter the monastery, I have no intention of ever coming out. I do not want all this money, and I want to help others. Actually, it will be God helping them, not me, because He has given me the means and He is to receive the glory."

Howard shook his head. He found it very hard to understand this daughter of his, but he would do his best to fulfill her wishes.

The lawyer, on the other hand, found all kinds of loopholes in her thinking. He tried everything he knew to make her wait, but to no avail. She very patiently asked him, "Mr. Stetson, do you feel I am paying you enough to take care of this for me?" He looked sheepish as he got the message, and from then on, all went smoothly.

Ellen met them for lunch after the appointment. "How did everything go?"

"Wonderful," Sarah said as she kissed her on the cheek. "It all went so well, and now, I have no money." She smiled and calmly looked at them. "How about buying a poor girl some lunch?"

They all laughed as they reached for each other's hands.

Chapter 35

August twenty-fourth arrived. Special permission had been granted for the wedding to take place. Usually, Catholic weddings are not performed on Sunday. Sarah felt it was a blessing that their birthday this year fell on the Lord's day.

Sheila's house was filled with family and friends.

As the sun rose and Sarah opened her eyes, she breathed a prayer of thanksgiving. Then she lay in bed in utter peace, letting the thoughts of the last few days envelop her. How close the families had become. She would never be able to thank God enough. When Ernest and Carmen had arrived, the night before last, Sheila, Howard, Ellen, Richard, Steve, all of them, had greeted them as though they had always been a part of their family. What amazed Sarah the most was seeing how Ellen truly admired her mother, and it thrilled her heart to see Carmen respond in the same way to Ellen. The two of them had gone shopping for their wedding dresses together and after dinner, they put on a fashion show for the rest of the family. Sarah smiled as she lay in bed and pictured them. She would spend the rest of her life thanking God for working all of this out and for preparing her way into Carmel.

With tears of happiness in her eyes, she thought of Sheila and how much enjoyment the last few weeks had been as they prepared for this day. They shopped together, shared together, laughed and cried together. She felt the tenderest emotions for her beloved sister and prayed to God to make her happy with Steve. To bless them with many children, and to let them be generous to those in need with the wealth God had provided for them.

She turned her head to look at the clock and was happy it was still early. She would stay in bed and continue reminiscing. . . .

A knock came on the door and, as she turned, Sheila was half-way through the room. "I am so glad that you are awake, too. I have been thinking of all the good things that have happened since we found each other and especially of the last few days."

Sarah smiled. "You do not have to tell me. I have a feeling they are the same thoughts and feelings I have had this morning."

Then they started sharing about Rome and all the blessings they received there. A knock came on the door and as the two of them turned to see who it was, Leah was halfway to the bed. "I knew you'd be awake. I want to get in on all this, too."

The three of them continued to share and laugh. The bed was shaking and they were, too, over the bicycle adventures in Europe and how they all felt staying in a convent. After awhile, Leah turned and looked at them. "I am so happy for both of you and I love you both very much." There was a touch of sadness in her voice.

The look the twins gave her more than told her how much they, too, loved her. Sarah reached for her hand. "Leah, God has something or someone planned for your life, too. Trust Him and remember, I will be praying every day for Him to care for you and give you happiness." All Leah could do was squeeze her hand in response.

The rest of the morning there was much hustle and bustle around the house. Martha had come over to help with the dinner, which would be served here after the wedding. This would be their last meal together as a family before they returned to the monastery at four p.m. for Sarah's entrance.

Ellen and Howard had often thought that when one of their daughters decided to marry, there would be such a large guest list they would not know where to hold the reception. Sheila, however, to Sarah's utter delight, decided she wanted a very small wedding, with only the family and very close friends. This way, after the wedding Mass at eleven a.m., they could return home and have a special dinner together. They needed to intimately share with only those closest to them. It would make all the more precious these last five hours before they accompanied Sarah back to the church and said their final good-byes to each other.

Chapter 36

The Carmelite chapel looked so beautiful to Sheila as she stood in the back, ready to walk down the aisle. Steve did not look a bit nervous as he stood in front, waiting for Mass to begin and for his bride to start toward him.

Father William and Father George were concelebrating. The music started and Leah sang, "On This Day, O Beautiful Mother" as Howard and Sheila started down the aisle. Sheila was radiant, as was Sarah, who followed behind as the maid of honor. It was startling to see how the twins were so identical; except for the different dresses, you could not tell them apart.

Most of the guests and family, and even the extern sisters in the convent found themselves holding their breath as they observed the twin sisters.

Father William smiled as he pronounced them man and wife and watched as they turned to each other. He admired Sarah's serenity as he saw the smile that lighted her face. He turned toward his own sister, Sister Agnes, their eyes met and they knew they were both thanking God.

Dinner at Steve and Sheila's house was a triumph for Martha, as she had prepared the twins' favorite meal. After dinner, everyone wanted to take more pictures. Most of them went to the sun parlor for this. The four parents found themselves alone.

"Well," Ernest said. "Before long it will be Sarah's turn."

Ellen instinctively looked at her watch. "How do you both feel about this? I still find it hard to accept."

Carmen looked up quickly. "How do you feel about Sheila getting married?"

"Well, I'm happy—I know Steve is a good man and they will have a good life together."

Carmen went over and sat next to Ellen. She looked at her intently. "Feel the same for Sarah. Know she has chosen the 'best man'." Then she looked at all of them, as she continued. "This has been such a blessed day and now, as we all go with Sarah to the monastery, there will be mixed feelings of emotion. We will not be able to help feeling both happy and sad, but remember, it is the emotion of the moment. As each day passes, we will know, more than ever, that Sarah is as close to us as she always was."

Sarah had slipped back into the room and was listening. She went over to them now and put her arm around each of them. "Be happy, all of you, but most of all, be yourselves. I want you all to know how much I love you. I, too, will have some sadness as I part from you, but my joy will be ever present."

Sarah was happy that she came back into the room and spent her last hour in the world outside the convent with her parents, all four of them.

Chapter 37

Sarah looked at herself in the mirror. She liked the new simple white dress she had chosen to wear. Carmen had gone to her room as she made these final preparations before leaving. She smiled now as she watched Sarah looking at herself. Sarah, who saw her, smiled back. Before they knew it, they were in each other's arms.

"Be sure Daddy knows how much I love him and thank him for all he has done for me."

"He knows, dear, he knows, as I do, how much you love us. You have been a gift from heaven for us, a blessing for which we will be forever thankful."

They pulled apart, still smiling at each other. "Well, mamacita, it is time. The time has finally come." With that, Sarah picked up her small bag and they left the room together. She laughed out loud as she saw the rest of the family waiting for her. "Don't look so grim. I'm not dying; I'm entering the monastery." In her natural way, she had everyone excited as they got into cars to follow her to the monastery.

Sarah drove with Steve and Sheila. When they got out of the car, they were right in front of the chapel. As they all stood and talked for a few minutes, Sarah explained, "After the sister meets me at the cloister door and I enter, you can all come back to the chapel. When I am in my habit, they will open the curtains and you will be able to see me for a few minutes, and I will see you." Her smile was radiant as she hugged them.

Then Richard put his arm around her waist and the two of them walked together up the paved road toward the cloister door. He was visibly shaken; this was a special time for the two of them. The rest of the family followed. At the door, Sarah turned to look at each of them. Then she went from one to the other, kissing and hugging. She turned to Sheila and they embraced. Sheila did not want to let her go, but Howard gently broke them apart and Steve took Sheila in his arms. Sarah hugged and kissed Howard and Ellen and finally stood before her father and mother, who were filled with tears but also with happy smiles.

"Will you give me your blessing, Daddy?" Ernest blessed his child as she knelt before him and then she embraced Ernest and Carmen together. She kissed her mother, then quickly turned and walked to the cloister door. She knocked three light taps on it. The door opened, and Sarah slipped inside. The nun shut the door behind her.

Silence fell on everyone as they stared at the door. Then Ernest put his arm around Carmen and they started down toward the church. Everyone followed them in complete silence. In the chapel, they either sat or knelt, prayed or thought, and waited.

The nuns started singing and, as the family watched, the curtain opened, and Sarah stood behind the grille, dressed in her habit. She looked beautiful. Tears lightly flowed down her cheeks as she saw them all. Ernest couldn't help but let a few sobs escape audibly. He couldn't hold them in. Carmen held him close as she, too, felt the stinging tears and the suppressed sobs filling her throat.

The curtain closed and the singing came to an end. Ernest and all of the family wiped their tears, genuflected and left the church.

Sarah, now Sister Michael Raphael of the Holy Angels, left the chapel and smiled as she walked into the room with Mother and all the sisters. Her new family made her feel very welcome and loved. Mother smiled and had no need to say anything as she took Sarah's hands and their eyes met.

Once outside the church, Sheila turned to her mother and father. She felt complete peace and happiness now. "Sarah wanted me to know from behind the grille how happy she is. We looked right into each other's eyes. I believe we both felt a complete release, yet with even stronger love and unity of mind and heart. It is hard to explain, but I know we both felt the same thing, as though we were one and always would be. We will now find our happiness, each in our own chosen vocation. We know this is not the end, only the beginning for both of us. We will be visiting her every month. She will not miss out on anything that happens in the family. We will all fill her in when we visit and make her a part of our lives, even though she lives in a cloistered convent." The family listened quietly as she spoke.

Ernest and Carmen felt touched by her words. Ellen and Howard looked tired, but relieved. She held Howard's hand and looked at him. "I, too, feel very peaceful now. It will still take us some time to understand all of this, but it was far easier to accept than I thought it would be. I know I will have many more tears and I thank God we will be able to visit her once a month, when possible." They stood in front of the church, sharing their innermost thoughts and feelings. There was more excitement as they waved good-bye to the newlyweds who drove off to start out on their honeymoon. The Farrell family said good-bye to the Montoyas. They were going to stay another day in Santa Fe before leaving for home.

Ernest and Carmen climbed into their old truck and headed out for Velarde. They held hands for most of the trip. It was an exhausting day but one that they would never forget. They could not help but reminisce about Sarah and the happy moments of her childhood and young adult life. They found themselves crying, and then laughing. Carmen sat close to him and could feel his strength which made it easier for her. As they pulled into their driveway, their hands instinctively tightened as they stared in disbelief at what was in front of them.

Neither of them said a word as they slid out of the old truck. They walked in front of it and reached once again for each other's hands as they continued to look at the magnificent, brand-new truck parked in their driveway. They turned to look at each other and burst out laughing. Then, once again, they looked at the truck and the huge cardboard smiley face looking out at them from the back window. Carmen gasped and her hands flew to cover her mouth. Her eyes twinkled as she whispered, "Sarah, you did it."

They walked around, got in the new truck, and said a prayer for Sarah. Their prayer was filled with laughter and they reached for each other and kissed. Carmen laid her head on Ernest's shoulder and neither of them seemed ready to get out of the truck and go in the house. All they could do was think of Sarah.

Right about this time, Sarah was in her new cell—the name of her small bedroom in the convent—she looked out the window as the sun was setting and laughed out loud.

She pictured her parents pulling into the driveway, and the expressions on their faces when they saw what she had done. She could feel their excitement and pleasure. These thoughts filled her with joy.

She knelt and gave honor and glory to God.

As she poured forth adoration to Him, her heart sang: "Taste and see the goodness of the Lord."

"Taste and see the goodness of the Lord."

THE END

coming soon sequel to The Lost Years *by Petra A. Bennett*

Title Description of Books by CMJ Associates, inc.

Behold the Man, Simon of Cyrene By Father Martin DePorres

Inspired writing by a gifted new Author. This story shows us the gifts given to Simon. Through carrying the Cross with Jesus, Simon shares with us the gifts we can expect by carrying our daily crosses.

Price $12.25 each

Becoming the Handmaid of the Lord By Dr. Ronda Chervin

The journals of this well known Catholic writer span her family life as wife and mother, mystical graces sustaining her through a mid-life crisis, the suicide of her beloved son, her widowhood and finally a Religious Sister at the age of 58. Insightful, inspiring & challenging. 327 pages of the heart.

Price $13.75 each

Ties that Bind By Ronda Chervin

The story of a Marriage. This beautiful novel presents the wife's point of view and the husbands point of view on the same conflict. The author Dr. Chervin has written many books on Catholic life. Ties that Bind is both funny and inspiring. A great gift for couple thinking about marriage as well.

Price $8.50 each

The Cheese Stands Alone By David Craig

(The formost religious poet of the day) A dynamite account of a radical conversion from the world of drugs to the search for holiness in the Catholic Church. Realism & poetic imagery combine to make this a must for those who want the real thing. Its a rare book that both monastic and charismatic — anyone acquainted with the latter will love the chapter on misguided zeal, aptly titled "Busbey Burkeley."

Price $12.50 each

The History of Eucharistic Adoration By Father John Hardon, s.j.

In an age of widespread confusion and disbelief, this document offers unprecedented clarity in the most important element of our faith. I recommend that it be prayerfully studied and widely circulated. It is thoroughly researched and well documented, and promises to enlighten, instruct and inspire countless souls to an undying love of our Eucharistic Lord.

Price $4.00 each

The Bishop Sheen We Knew By Father Albert Shamon

A booklet filled with little known information from his Vicar, Fr. Albert J.M. Shamon, Bishop Dennis Hickey and Fr. Mike Hogan, the three remaining priests who worked under Bishop Sheen. A chance to see the day to day workings of the acknowledged prophet of our times.

Price $4.00 each

Born, Unborn By Martin Chervin

What if inside this hospital bag, smashed in pieces, crushed to bits, evidence to make one believe God didn't exist. What if, a second time on earth, the Spirit of Mercy was giving birth, end of the voyage down to earth. In this bag, the child Christ returning to us... A second time, crucified.

Price $9.95 each

To order additional copies of this book:

Please complete the form below and send for each copy
CMJ Marian Publishers
P.O. Box 661 • Oak Lawn, IL 60454
call toll free 888-636-6799 or fax 708-636-2855
email jwby@aol.com
www.cmjbooks.com

Name _____

Address _____

City _____ State _____ Zip _____

Phone (   ) _____

	QUANTITY	SUBTOTAL

Message to the World
$10.00   x   _____   = $ _____

Children of the Breath
$14.50   x   _____   = $ _____

Becoming the Handmaid of the Lord
$13.75   x   _____   = $ _____

Radiating Christ
$11.00   x   _____   = $ _____

The Cheese Stands Alone
$12.50   x   _____   = $ _____

The History of Eucharistic Adoration
$ 4.00   x   _____   = $ _____

The Bishop Sheen We Knew
$ 4.00   x   _____   = $ _____

Behold the Man!
$12.25   x   _____   = $ _____

_____

$__.__   x   _____   = $ _____

+ tax (for Illinois residents only)   = $ _____

+ 15% for S&H   = $ _____

TOTAL   = $ _____

☐ Check # _____   ☐ Visa   ☐ MasterCard

Exp. Date ___/___/___

Card # _____

_____
signature

Many new & exciting releases for Winter 1997

*(If you are interested in any or all of these exciting new titles send us
your name and address and we can send you a notice of publication with the price.)*

By Way of the Cross By Carol J. Ross

Autobiography. When you read By Way of the Cross you will open
yourself to tears of empathy and of joy as you see this woman strug-
gling with terribly physical and mental crosses, scooped up into
breathtaking visions of the supernatural world. Paperback. Full color
photos. 468 pages. $12.50

Lost in the World: Found in Christ By Father Christopher Scadron

The story of a priest ordained at the age of 63 — As a young Jewish
man Padre Pio predicated he would become a Priest. After years of
floundering and sin as a naval officer and an artist, this unusually
gifted and interested man became a priest at 63! A tale all Catholics
will find moving and deeply inspiring, it is also a must for any man
you know who might be called to the priesthood at an age older than
the usual. $12.50

Dancing with God through the Evening of Life
By Mary Anne McCrickard Benas

Unique insight into the world of the hospice worker and the patient
relationship. The beautiful faithful outlook of a elderly man dying
and the gifts he gives us through this experience. $12.50

The Third Millennium Woman By Patricia Hershwitzky

Consider the sinking feeling many Catholics get when they see litera-
ture about preparing for this great event. They expect what they read
or pretend to read to be true, but dull as dishwater. By contrast —
here is a book that is wildly funny and also profound. Written by a
"revert" (born Catholic who left and then returned), it is also ideal as
a gift for those many women we know are teetering on the verge of
returning Home. $12.50

Messages to the World from the Mother of God

Daily meditative pocketsize prayer book on the monthly messages
given the visionaries in Medjugorji for the conversion of the World,
back to her son Jesus. These messages for the World started in 1984
till the present. In 1987 the messages began on the 25th of the month
(union of two hearts with the 5 wounds of Jesus) thus the 25th. These
are from St. James Church in Medjugorji. Great Gift!!! $10.00

Children of the Breath By Martin Chervin

Who would have dared to challenge Creation if, at the close of each
new day, God said, "It is perfect." Instead, His lips spoke "It is good. .
." and the serpent was already in Eden. Thus begins Children of the
Breath, a startling journey into the desert where Christ was tempted
for forty days of darkness and light. With immense clarity, lyricism,
and humor, author Martin Chervin has delivered a powerhouse that
will engage readers of any faith. $14.50

Radiating Christ By Fr. Raoul Plus, S.J.

To be a "Christ" is the whole meaning of Christianity. To radiate
Christ is the whole meaning of the Christian apostolate. But to be a
Christ for one's own personal benefit is not enough; we have to
Christianize those around us; in a word we have to radiate Christ. $11.00

To order additional copies of this book:

Please complete the form below and send for each copy
CMJ Marian Publishers
P.O. Box 661 • Oak Lawn, IL 60454
call toll free 888-636-6799 or fax 708-636-2855
email jwby@aol.com
www.cmjbooks.com

Name _____

Address _____

City _____ State _____ Zip _____

Phone (   ) _____

                                   QUANTITY   SUBTOTAL

Message to the World
         $10.00   x   _____   = $ _____

Children of the Breath
         $14.50   x   _____   = $ _____

Becoming the Handmaid of the Lord
         $13.75   x   _____   = $ _____

Radiating Christ
         $11.00   x   _____   = $ _____

The Cheese Stands Alone
         $12.50   x   _____   = $ _____

The History of Eucharistic Adoration
         $ 4.00   x   _____   = $ _____

The Bishop Sheen We Knew
         $ 4.00   x   _____   = $ _____

Behold the Man!
         $12.25   x   _____   = $ _____

_____

         $__.__   x   _____   = $ _____

         + tax (for Illinois residents only)   = $ _____

         + 15% for S&H   = $ _____

         TOTAL   = $ _____

☐ Check # _____   ☐ Visa   ☐ MasterCard

                                          Exp. Date ___/___/___

Card # _____

_____
                                        signature